# ENTICED BY A KINGPIN 2

## BOOK 2

### MIA BLACK

D1569090

## CHAPTER 1

The last few hours had been some of the craziest of my life. I didn't know how one day could become so chaotic but that was the only word for it as far as I was concerned. I'd been trying to calm my mind so that I could think clearly but I was too panicked to really do so.

Miles and I had been in Miami for the better part of a week. It was amazing to spend time with him and more importantly to get away from the hospital. I slaved away there every day so it was nice to have time to relax. Miles and I finally had sex with one another and it was everything that I'd hoped it would be. We even made it official and became a real couple. We were both on cloud nine as we made our way back to Chicago and back to real life.

Everything had been going smoothly with us. Miles had parked his car at the airport before we left so we'd gone and picked it up so he could drive us home. The police ended up pulling us over and before I knew it, Miles was being taken away in handcuffs while I was trying to find a way home with the money that he'd stuffed in my purse before they took him.

Stella had come to pick me up a little while later since they took Miles' car. I was glad for it at first but the tension between the two of us was thick as we sat in my condo. She was on the verge of scolding me like a child for even being with Miles and I was such an emotional wreck that I didn't want to deal with it right then.

"So, what next?" I asked. One of Miles' guys had text me from some number and told me to open the door. He'd asked for the money that Miles had given to me.

"He'll contact you," was all he said before he turned and headed towards the elevator. I called after him trying to get more information but he just kept on moving. I was annoyed with it because I wanted to know how they planned on getting Miles out of jail.

I turned back to Stella, who had a confused but serious look on her face. I explained to her what happened and she was also wondering what the money was for. It wasn't until we'd sat thinking about it for a few more minutes that I realized that it was most likely going to be used for Miles' bail, which was why he gave it to me.

Stella stayed with me for a little while longer but she needed to get home and get some sleep herself. I thanked her for coming and let her know that I'd keep her updated, even though I didn't really plan on it. I was starting to feel some kind of way about Stella and how she felt about Miles' and I relationship.

Three days had gone by slowly and I still hadn't heard from Miles. I was trying my hardest not to go crazy but it was hard not to. Miles and I had a real connection with one another. I had become so used to spending time with him that it was difficult not to be around him. I was worried about his wellbeing. I didn't know if he was still locked up or not but I needed answers and didn't know how to go about getting them.

All of my worries about Miles had made it clear to me just how much I really cared about him. In fact, I'd realized that I had somehow fallen in love with him. I knew what he did for a living was scary but that wasn't who he was as a person, at least not in his heart. The Miles that I knew was smart, sweet, and a romantic. He'd been nothing but great to me, always having my back and listening to me when I wanted to talk. There was something special about him.

I was at home on my day off, trying to take a nap when my phone rang. I didn't recognize the number, but I answered anyway. When the computerized voice came on telling me that I had a call from a corrections facility, I automatically accepted it, knowing who it had to be on the other end.

"Miles?" I answered. I sat up in the bed, moving to the edge of it and crossing my legs.

"Are you alright?" That was the first thing that he said to me. Here it was that he was calling me from jail and his first concern was me. "Them cops ain't hurt you or nothing, right?"

I shook my head as though he could see me. "No. They let me go right after they took you away. I had Stella come and pick me up. Enough about me. What happened with you? When are you getting out? I tried to ask your friend about it but he wouldn't tell me anything. I don't wanna be in the dark anymore, Miles." I'd missed talking to him for sure, but I hoped that this situation showed him that I was more than just a girlfriend and that I was really a ride or die.

"Calm down," he said in a low voice. "It's alright. I'm sorry for all that. I'm just tryin' to keep you safe. I don't want you involved in this stuff. That's why I'm only calling you now."

"What does that mean?"

"I'm about to be released. My people posted my bail. I'm waiting for them to come and pick me up. The guards are about to process me," he explained.

I got up off the bed and started looking for my sneakers. "I'm about to leave in a few minutes. I'll get a cab and be there in a few."

"Kallie, don't come," he said. His voice was dead serious.

I stopped moving around the room. "What do you mean, don't come?" I asked.

"There's a lot goin' on," Miles responded. "There's things happening with my life you don't know about. I just wanna keep you away from all of it so just chill out, please. The less you know the easier for you."

"I'm not trying to hear all that. I'll see you in a few," I said. I hung up the phone before he had a chance to argue with me some more. I knew what he wanted from me, but he needed to realize that I was more than some woman he was messing with. I was his girl and I cared about him.

I decided to drive my own car to pick up Miles instead of taking a cab. I wanted us to be able to talk freely and we wouldn't have privacy with someone else driving the car. I did a quick search online for the location of the place that Miles had called from. Once I had that, I was on my way there.

The corrections building was huge and gray, but the processing part was much smaller. I imagined that not too many people were coming in and out of the jail on a daily basis. I hated that Miles had even been in there for so long.

When I pulled up, Miles was standing outside. He was wearing the same clothes that he'd had on when we first came back from Miami. He didn't look too happy when he saw me. I knew he had to be upset since he'd specifically told me not to come but he couldn't have thought that I'd actually listen to him.

I was walking up to him when another called pulled up behind mine. The familiar black truck came to a stop and two guys got out, both of them being faces that I recognized as Miles' people. I gave Miles a kiss on the cheek and he hugged me tightly for a few seconds before telling me he needed to go talk to his friends. After a few minutes he came back over to me

"I'm gonna ride with you, but they're gonna follow us," he explained. I nodded my head and made my way back over to my car. Miles got in the passenger seat and rolled his window down.

"Miles, why did the cops take you in?" I asked as we pulled up at a stop light. I hated the fact that I was blind in the situation with him. I couldn't really do anything besides ask questions and hope that I'd get a straight answer.

"Why'd you come and pick me up, Kallie?" He turned to me with frustration on his face. "I told you not to come."

"Don't try and flip this on me," I countered. "I haven't heard anything from you for three days. You send your guys to my house to come and get money and even they don't tell me anything. I was worried. What else was I supposed to do? You're not telling me anything."

"Don't you think there's probably a reason for that?" He growled.

"We're not going back to this whole keeping secrets thing, Miles," I shot back. "Stop thinking that you can protect me from everything by keeping me away from it."

"But the cops are involved now," he argued.

"So what? I just saw you get arrested. I'm not as immune to this stuff as you think. I could have been taken away too. You had no way of knowing that," I said.

"Kallie, this ain't your world. This shit is real life," he tried to reason with me. I was focused on the road, but I could feel his eyes on me.

I took a deep breath. "Miles, did you forget all the stuff that I told you about my life growing up?" My voice had gotten a little softer as I tried to calm my emotions. "I'm *from* Chicago, I didn't just move here. You keep thinking that you're protecting me but in reality, ain't none of this stuff new. You know I don't know people in gangs? You know I don't know shooters? You think *I've* never held a gun? I'm not saying I'm about to be Bonnie to your Clyde running the streets with you, but I can handle more than you think I can. I just need to know what to handle."

Miles didn't say anything for a little bit. I could tell that he was thinking hard about what I'd just said to him. I was being as honest as I could though. I needed him to see me as an asset to him and not someone that needed to be looked after.

"I'm being watched," Miles said after a while.

"By who?"

He shook his head. "I don't know."

"So how do-?"

"The cops got somebody on the inside," he answered before I could finish. "I don't know who but somehow a lot of my information has been leaking."

"Is there a way to flush 'em out?" I asked.

He shook his head again. "Not at this moment," he sighed. "The cops are trying to pin murders on me and people that we didn't even do. We've been trying to lay low but it's hard cause we're at war. The cops don't care though. They just wanna lock somebody up so they can say they did their jobs."

"That's how it is sometimes," I said. "But you just have to be smart about the way you do things. Play it all close to the chest."

He nodded with understanding. "Yeah," was all he managed to say.

"Thank you for telling me." I reached out and grabbed his hand in mine, locking up our fingers. "It means a lot to me. I'm here for you however you need me to be."

"I know," Miles held my hand up to his mouth and kissed it.

We got to my apartment and I parked the car. It didn't seem like Miles was leaving anytime soon since the black truck that followed us was now parked across the street from my apartment.

In the elevator on the way up Miles was acting like a teenager. He couldn't keep his hands off of me, rubbing on my thigh or trying to feel me up over my clothes. It had only been three days since we'd last seen one another but I guessed that going from having sex every day to not getting any had made him horny.

I unlocked the door to my apartment and before I could close it behind us all the way, Miles was on me. He was kissing all over the back of my neck and trying to loosen up my jeans.

"Miles, don't you think you should take a shower first?" I was horny now that I was with him again, but he'd also been in jail for a few days.

"Only if you're comin' with me," Miles said with a devilish smirk on his face.

Miles didn't even wait for me to say anything. He didn't take his eyes off of me as he stripped his clothes off. His hoodie and shirt came over his head in one fluid motion. He kicked off his shoes and socks with ease. Slowly he undid his pants and let them fall to the floor along with his underwear. Naked as the day he was born, Miles turned around and headed towards the bathroom barefoot. It felt like the temperature in the room had gone up a few degrees as I watched his muscular back and firm ass walk.

I had been missing my man for days and now that he'd come back I wasn't about to miss an opportunity to be with him. I moved quick, stripping off my clothes until I was naked and then walking quickly towards the bathroom.

Miles had already turned on the water when I got inside. The steam was only starting to fill up the room. I stepped into the shower to find Miles standing under the warm water with his eyes closed. I had to take a moment to admire him as I watched the water cascade down his muscular, tattooed body.

I knew that there was probably more that we needed to talk about, but I put it all aside. I knew it was only three days, but Miles had been locked inside of a cell and couldn't move the way that he wanted to. I didn't want to add on more stress.

I walked up to him and kissed him gently on the lips. He added more force and the kiss became more passionate. The droplets of water splashed off of his body.

I grabbed a washcloth and took my time lathering him up with soap. The vanilla scent of it mixed with the real making the whole bathroom smell like it. Miles was enjoying me washing him but he couldn't keep his hands off me either. His big hands were massaging whatever parts of my body he could get to.

Finally, he couldn't take it anymore. He turned me around and pressed me against the wall. I could feel his hardness poking my backside as his head bent down closer to me and started to bite and suck on my neck.

"Ooh," I let out a moan. I propped one of my feet up on the side of the shower to give him a better angle.

Miles slowly slid himself inside of me, taking his time, inch by inch. I reached behind me and put my hand on his head as he moved from one side to another on my neck. Once he'd pushed himself all the way in, he put his hands on both sides of my hips and slowly started to pull me back on to him.

I hadn't had sex in the shower in years, so I'd forgotten just how intense it could be. The moment was only intensified by the water pouring off of us. The sounds of it mixed with the noises of Miles' body slapping against mine. He was hammering away at me, slamming my body back onto his faster and faster.

"Damn, I missed this shit!" Miles exclaimed as he palmed my breasts in his hands. I was moving on my own now, throwing it back on his firm frame.

"Me too," I moaned.

"Fuck!" Miles let out. He slammed his hand against the wall as he pulled himself out of me. He was breathing hard moaning a little bit still as he used his hand to finish himself off, letting his seed drop onto the floor of the tub as the water quickly washed it away.

I turned around to Miles, still feeding off of his sexual energy and kissed him on the lips again passionately. I grabbed the washcloth again, this time to clean us up for real.

A few minutes later the two of us were laying in my bed. Miles was on his side and I was laying facing him. Our legs were wrapped up in each other and his arm was laid over my waist.

I was rubbing my hand up and down his muscled arm as I started talking to him. "Miles, I was so scared when the cops took you away. I didn't know what I'd do. I thought they were gonna come and take me too." The situation with the cops had been heavy on my mind for a few days.

"I'm sorry that you had to go through all that," he said as he leaned in closer and pecked me on the lips. "You know how much I wanna keep you safe. I don't know what I would've done if something happened to you."

"It wasn't your fault," I replied. I knew that he was feeling guilt over the situation but there was nothing that he could do about it.

Miles put his hand on my chin to make sure I was focused on him. The look in his eyes was serious. "You need to leave me alone. That way you won't get wrapped up in any of my stuff."

"So what are you saying? You wanna break up with me? We just got together," I replied. I knew that he was in his own head with worry over the situation, but I felt like we'd just talked about this in the car on the way here.

He took a deep breath. "I'm not saying it's what I want, but I *am* saying that it might be for the best," he shot back.

I shook my head defiantly. "Miles, I'm already in too deep. I'm with you. I understand what you're saying but all it means is that I need to be careful."

"Kallie, I don't want anything to happen to you," he said softly. "I'd go crazy."

"Nothing's gonna happen. I promise," I replied as I stroked his face gently.

## CHAPTER 2

It felt like a wall had been broken down between Miles and I after he got out of jail. I guessed that it was my insistence on him being more honest with me, but he was taking my words to heart and it was making the two of us get closer.

There were times when it was just the two of us and Miles would tell me stuff about him. Sometimes it would be stories about himself and how he grew up. Other times they'd be about the people that he kept around him; how they'd joined up with him or what they did. He kept a lot of things very general, preferring not to go into details too often. He also gave me the big picture of what was happening with his situation on the streets.

In finding out more about Miles and the way that he actually lived, I discovered more about the way he thought. Because of his lifestyle and the current war that he was involved in, he didn't go anywhere with security. The men that went around with him were his lieutenants, but they also acted as security. Miles was smart because he also had security with him that didn't look like they were doing their job. I'd tried a couple of times to spot them when we were out, but he explained that he paid them a lot of money to make sure that no one could tell they were there.

I also learned just how much of a boss Miles was. He was young, but old in terms of street years. Sadly, a lot of people from where we were from didn't make it to see 25. It was a consequence of staying involved in the game.

Miles explained to me one night how he'd made it to where he was. He'd started off as a drug runner at a young age. He'd be the one to make the final transaction and if the cops came it was his job to take the drugs and run. He slowly worked his way up in the organization by proving his loyalty and paying attention to how the old heads did things. Once he saw an opportunity, he took it. He started off small with just a block but soon his empire grew until he owned the majority of the territory. In fact, the only people above him were the connects themselves. He explained that because he did good business and showed respect, he got it in return from the connects. They were able to help him out with protection because they knew he could be trusted and didn't want someone else to take his place that they didn't know.

For a while I struggled with the morality of the situation. I had dedicated my life to being a doctor and I knew that in doing so, I was trying to help people and do good in the world. That conflicted with knowing what Miles did for a living because I knew that violence couldn't really be avoided in his lifestyle.

One night when we were in my apartment I brought this up to him. I explained how I felt and just like always he sat and listened to me. When I was done, he let me know his stance on violence.

Miles considered himself to be a thinker. He told me that while he has had to hurt people before, it's not his go to, nor is it something that he advises his people to do. It was contrary to everything that you heard on the news about Chicago, but Miles said he'd always instructed his crew to only use violence if it was necessary. He preferred for them to outthink the competition, rather than outgun them.

He also explained that a lot of times he could avoid situations in general because he had a whole other network of people under his employ. He paid the police, judges, the D.A., anyone that could help him to get rid of his competition legally. He said that it was a win-win situation because they got the glory for taking down drug dealers and he got to continue running his business in peace.

*I'm here.*

The text came through to my phone not a moment too soon. I was at the hospital doing a double. Miles had hit me up earlier in the day asking whether I wanted to do lunch or not. He suggested that we have it at the hospital since it had become one of our normal meeting spots. I told him I was down and asked him to let me know when he'd arrived so I could take my break.

As Miles and I got closer, I wanted to make certain things clear to him. I thought they'd be important to help out the both of us. I told him in no uncertain terms that I didn't want any of his "business" at my apartment. That meant no drugs and no drama. He looked at me like I was dumb, reminding me that *he* was the one trying to keep me safe, not the other way around.

I stepped into the hospital's huge cafeteria and scanned the room for Miles. I spotted him off to the left-hand side sitting close to a wall. He waved me over when he saw me, so I walked over to him. He stood when he saw me, grabbing me in his arms and hugging me tightly before kissing me on the cheek. I didn't want to have the public display of affection in the hospital, so we kept it light.

"How's your day going?" Miles asked as I took my seat across from him. "I got you a sandwich. It's one of those chicken pesto joints that you like."

"Thanks," I smiled. "Work is cool. It's just a long ass shift. How's your day been?"

"Quiet," he responded. "But I don't know if that's a good thing or a bad thing. I'm here now though so I got a little while to breathe."

The times that Miles and I spent together had to be structured in a weird way because of all the stuff he was going through with his other life. Miles was incredibly cautious so he either came to my house after dark, or we'd just head outside of the city to enjoy ourselves. The hospital had become a favorite place to meet because it was safe. No one was going to follow him there and if his phone was tapped the way he believed it to be, it was safe for Miles to talk about heading to "follow up" doctor's appointments, which in reality were just meetings with me. There were a lot of secrets and shadows shrouding Miles but I was finding ways to get through or around them.

"What you got planned for later on?" I asked him.

He looked like he was thinking as he squinted his eyes and looked away from me. "Today? I gotta go check on some of my people. I asked them to do something for me and I wanna check in person that it got done."

"Oh, ok, cool," I responded. "I wish I could come over later, but this shift is so damn long."

"I know." He took a sip of the coffee he'd

ordered for himself. "I was thinking about that too."

"So, have you spoken to your friend yet?" Miles asked. He folded his arms across his chest and looked at me with a questioning glance.

I sighed and took a sip of water. "Not really. But I know that I need to."

Miles was asking about Stella. Because my relationship with Miles took up most of my time outside of work, I didn't really have time to spend with Stella the way that I used to. I missed talking to her and being around her, but it wasn't as simple as it once was. Our relationship was strained and it had nothing to do with spending time together.

Stella had made it clear to me on several occasions that she didn't approve of my relationship with Miles. It had hurt me to know it was true, so much that I even told Miles about it one night when we were in bed together. He knew how much I cared about her and our friendship, so he'd been encouraging me to try talking some sense into her. I'd been meaning to try but I hadn't really been seeing her too often. When we did see one another, we kept it at a professional level as if we were being forced to.

It was kind of uncomfortable, but I knew that we probably just needed a girls night out or something to get back on track.

"I'm only asking for you," Miles said. "I could care less how she feels about me, but that's your friend. You don't wanna mess up a friendship over something dumb."

I nodded with understanding. "Yeah, I know. I'm gonna try and talk to her."

The truth of the matter was that I believed Stella's issue with Miles had less to do with me and more to do with her. Stella had been dropping little hints every now and then about what kind of person she believed Miles to be. I could deal with that for the most part because I understood the perception of people involved in his lifestyle.

The issue was that I believed that Stella was jealous of Miles and I on some levels. Miles had money, I didn't know how much, but he never let me take care of the bill, even though I had more than enough of my own to do so. Beyond having money, he was also incredibly generous with it. He bought me gifts and sent stuff to the hospital for me all the time: flowers, chocolates, cards, the works. Whenever I'd get something,

Stella would always have some comment to say about it or where the money was coming from. The truth was that I believed she was jealous on some level. Stella had no problems getting a man but keeping one for more than a little while was something she didn't do. I knew she would probably try and dismiss it all as her not wanting one, but in all honesty, I was starting to realize that they just didn't take her seriously

Miles and I sat with each other for my entire lunch break. He was always just the distraction that I needed from dealing with my patients. Sometimes, some of them could be incredibly difficult. A lot of times I'd deal with racists or perverts who had issues with taking advice from a woman, let alone a black one. I was just glad to be able to push all of that out of my mind.

Miles had just left. I was cleaning up the table that we'd sat at when I felt someone tap me on the shoulder. I turned around to see it was Stella. She was looking gorgeous as usual with her light brown and blonde curls cascading down to her shoulders.

"Hey girl." I greeted her with a smile. It quickly left my face once I realized she was only half smirking back at me.

"Hey," she said flatly.

"What's your problem?" I asked. I didn't know if Stella had seen me with Miles or not. She'd walked up to me after he was already gone but I could tell by her demeanor that she was upset about something.

Stella took a deep breath. "Kallie, how the hell can you sit in this hospital and have lunch with that man? You know all the shit he's responsible for." Her voice had an ice-cold edge to it as she rudely spoke to me. I put the tray that was in my hands down so I could turn my whole body to her.

"Stella, you don't know what you're talking about," I answered. I took a step closer to her as I nervously looked around. "And keep your voice down."

"Like hell I don't," she shot back, although in a quieter tone.

I wasn't backing down either. "It's really clear to me that you have an issue with Miles and if this how you gonna act, I'm not gonna talk to you about him. You're out here making assumptions about things you don't know about."

"I'm not Stupid, Kallie," Stella responded.

"You called *me*, when he got arrested, remember?" Stella stopped talking and motioned for me to sit down. There was a lot of tension between us, but I did.

When she spoke again, Stella's voice had changed. She didn't sound so upset but she still reminded me of a parent chastising a child. "We see so many people come in here on a daily basis that have been victims of the violence this city is known for. I can't believe that you're out here spreading your legs for the man that's probably responsible for it. The dick must be good."

I sat back in shock. If anyone had told me a while ago that Stella and I would be at one another's throats the way that we were, I'd have called them a liar. I just knew that Stella was my friend and had been for years. But now I was seeing another side of her and I didn't like it one bit.

"Don't make assumptions when you're on the outside looking in," I shot back. "I know Miles. You don't. You don't know shit about him besides what I tell you."

"I don't need to know that man to know the type of man he is," she argued.

I leaned forward and had to restrain myself from holding my finger out in her face. "You don't know what the fuck you're talking about and you need to leave this alone. Why don't you focus on finding yourself a man to last longer than two weeks instead of being so pressed over mine?"

Stella leaned back in her chair, clearly taken aback by my words. "Wow, I'm just trying to help you out and be a friend. But if that's how you feel, there's nothing else for me to say. Mark my words though, Kallie. That man is gonna bring you down and when he does, I don't want you coming crawling back to me."

I opened my mouth to speak but I was too flustered. I stormed away from the table, leaving Stella and my trash behind me. I tried to throw myself into work for the rest of the day, but I was too distracted. I couldn't believe that Stella had come at me the way that she did. I was beyond thinking she was just trying to help. I already worried enough about Miles when he was doing what he did and now I'd lost my best friend over it.

## CHAPTER 3

I 'd been Stella's friend for years so I knew that she could be a lot to handle when she was upset. The thing about the situation between the two of us was that neither one of us were backing down. We both could be adult enough to admit when we were wrong but in this case, neither of us could see the forest for the trees. She believed she was just trying to help me out and I was of the mindset that if that was help, I didn't want to see what her hurt was like.

The situation was only further complicated by the fact that she was also my boss. I was a member of her team so a lot of my direction came from her. It had been a few days of us not speaking to one another outside of work stuff and it was making the situation difficult.

As anyone who's ever been on any kind of team could tell you, you needed to be on one accord. That especially held true for medical teams. I was starting to notice petty stuff being done. When I'd come up with a diagnosis, she'd argue against it, even if it seemed like I was right. My schedule even got worse because Stella had taken it upon herself to schedule me for more time in the clinic. I hated doing clinic duty. I didn't want to spend my time wiping running noses and bandaging up children when there was real work to be done upstairs.

I felt so strongly about it that I'd even confronted her about it one day. She was at a nurses' station by herself, so I decided it would be the perfect time to approach.

"Stella?" I called out to her as I made my way to her.

"Yes Dr. Jameson?" Her tone was ice cold and she didn't even look up from the screen that she was typing away at. It was like she was trying to give me the least amount of attention possible.

I didn't let her attitude faze me. "I'm scheduled to do the last four hours of my shift on clinic duty. I spoke to Dr. Smith and he's willing to cover for me so I can finish up with my patients up here."

Stella finally stopped typing and turned her head slowly towards me as if she only just noticed I was there. "That's not gonna work for me," she said in a flat tone.

I was confused. There was never an issue with someone covering someone else's clinic duty before so I didn't understand it then. "Why not?"

"I scheduled *you* for the hours, Dr. Jameson, not Dr. Smith. I think you could use the experience."

"It's never been a problem before," I replied.

"That was before. This is after," she answered. I started to open my mouth to say something that would have shut her up but gotten me in trouble, but I decided not to. Instead I just grit my teeth and went about my day.

The tension between Stella and I was so bad that Ashley started to notice. One day after I'd just finished up with a patient, I was walking down the hall when she came up to me.

"Hey," Ashley said awkwardly. There wasn't much tension between us anymore but there wasn't really any friendship either. I wasn't holding a grudge for what had gone down between us before, but I also hadn't forgotten.

"Hey Ashley." I tried to sound casual.

I was glad when she decided to get straight to the point. "I don't wanna be nosy or anything like that, but is everything cool between you and Stella? It seems like you guys have been arguing a lot. People notice."

I assumed that by "people" she meant herself. I knew that it wouldn't be too long before someone else got wind. It wasn't hard to see. Stella and I had gone from talking all the time to not speaking at all. The issue was definitely bothering me and was on my mind all the time. I wasn't about to let Ashley know that though.

"Nah, we're cool." I brushed it off with a shrug. "We've just both been busy."

"Oh, ok." She seemed like didn't believe me but also didn't press the issue further. "Um...can I ask you something else?" Her voice had gotten a little quieter.

"Sure."

"Are you and Christian still a thing?" she asked. Her eyes were focused intently on mine as if she was about to see the answer before I said something.

I couldn't help but to let out a little laugh. I knew that she had ulterior motives. I guessed that when she decided to get up in my business, she decided to get all the way in.

"Look, if you wanna go back to sleeping with Christian, or if you've *already* gone back to sleeping with him, it's cool," I said. "I'm not with him and haven't been for a while."

I practically felt the energy come off of Ashley as she let out the breath that she'd been holding in. She plastered on a smile. "I just wanted to know."

"I bet," I said with a smirk.

I fully expected for Ashley to turn and leave now that she'd gotten the answers to her questions, but instead she struck up a conversation with me. I couldn't tell if it was because she wanted more information about something or if she was genuinely trying to be nice, but it was a welcome change.

Ashley and I ended up doing our rounds together. It was something that Stella and I would do sometimes. Sometimes patients felt more comfortable having two people around them. It was a benefit to me because I could have someone around to bounce ideas off of.

Stella spotted Ashley and me. I could tell by the look on her face that she was pissed. Her eyes were small and narrow, focused on Ashley and me as we chatted with one another. I knew what had to be going through her mind but since she wasn't talking to me I didn't really care.

Later on in the afternoon, Ashley was out on lunch while I was leaving a patient's room with a urine sample. This old woman had come in complaining about problems peeing. I needed the samples to figure out if it was just a bladder infection or something more serious with her kidneys. I'd also grabbed some vials of her blood to test those as well.

I walked into the testing room and set the containers down on the counter so I could get everything set up. I grabbed my gloves and was about to head back over to the samples when the door opened. Stella walked in and closed the door behind her. I'd already put on my goggles and was ready to do the tests, so I hoped she wasn't coming to me with any mess.

"I can't believe you, Kallie," Stella huffed. She also had some samples of her own and put them down on the counter. She folded her arms over her chest.

"What are you talking about?" I asked.

"What's up with you being friend with Ashley all of a sudden? I thought we'd agreed we weren't cool with her after the stunt she pulled before." Stella's eyes were lit up with anger.

Ashley had basically stolen a promotion from Stella. Stella had been putting in work trying to earn a higher position but had somehow been skipped over for it. We believed that it had everything to do with Ashley sleeping with Christian and him being a board member. She'd also found herself on my shit list over her insistence on trying to get between Christian and I back when we were a thing.

"I was talking to the woman. We're not best friends." I brushed off Stella's accusations. I wasn't about to forget everything that Ashley had done but I also wasn't about to let it ruin my life or anything.

I had tests that needed to be run so I politely moved myself around Stella and grabbed the blood samples that I needed to test. I put one of them into a machine that would help break it down and turned it on.

"So you're trying to tell me that I didn't see what I saw?" Stella asked. I was working on the urine sample now, grabbing the components I needed to test it out.

"Stella, could we not do this right now?" I was about to start the test and I needed to concentrate.

"You're supposed to be loyal to me," Stella said.

At that point I just couldn't' take it anymore. I put the sample back down and turned to her. "I am loyal, Stella," I responded. "You're the one whose turned their back on me. I've been nothing but a friend to you."

"And you think I haven't been one to you?" she countered. "All I was trying to do was help you out and tell you that you're making a mistake."

"And you've made your point," I said. "But you're just mad cause I'm not listening. News-flash: this isn't med school anymore. You can tell me what to do cause you're my boss but if you're gonna be my friend then you need to respect my decisions."

Stella shook her head. "I can't believe you," she responded. She turned and grabbed the patient samples that she'd come in with, leaving without another word.

Usually I was on top of my game. I tried to pay close attention to detail because it helped me out when it came to diagnosing patients. My argument with Stella had taken my already crowded day to another level. I finished running the tests on the patient and turned them in.

I was going about the rest of my day trying to just get through it so I could get home and drink a glass or five of wine. Fate had other plans as my day went from bad to worse. I was informed by a nurse that I'd been summoned up to HR. I ran through my entire day trying to think of a reason that they'd want to see me, but I couldn't find one.

When I got upstairs I headed to one of the Human Resource offices. I'd been up on this floor before due to the incident with Ashley. This time I was directed to another part, one that I recognized as the place that dealt with medical issues. I felt myself getting a lot more nervous.

I was greeted by a secretary who told me that Dr. Roberts was waiting for me. I walked into the large office with its light gray walls huge windows. Seated behind the desk was Dr. Roberts, one of the hospital administrators. She was an older woman in her 50's. She'd retired from medicine but still consulted on cases every now and then. She had caramel colored skin and a short pixie haircut that was black and gray. It showcased her round and beautiful face.

"Hello Kallie, have a seat," Dr. Roberts said. "I hope you don't mind me calling you by your first name. I find that it makes people feel more comfortable. You can call me Helen."

I took a seat in the large wood chair opposite her desk. I tried to smile but it didn't really work. "I'm sorry, Helen, but what's this all about?"

"Well, there was an error made today and we wanted to get to the bottom of it. I was hoping you'd be able to help me with that," she explained. Her tone was formal but still had a friendly edge to it.

"Sure. What's the issue?" I asked.

Helen pulled out a folder and handed it to me. I looked it over, recognizing it as the charts for one of my current patients. It was the woman that I'd been running tests on earlier in the day.

"Do you recognize this patient file?" Helen asked.

"Yes," I answered with a nod. "It's Josephine Stanley. I did a blood panel and ran a urine test. Her kidneys are malfunctioning."

"That in itself is the issue," Helen responded. "She reacted badly to a steroid that you gave her for her kidneys. It was because she didn't need the medicine. After we stabilized her, we reran the rests and it turns out all she needed were antibiotics for a kidney infection."

I opened my mouth to speak and then closed it. I was shocked. I couldn't believe that I'd made such a mistake. If it wasn't for Stella coming at me with her petty bullshit, I definitely wouldn't have messed up. I knew that she was distracting me. I shouldn't have even started the tests until she was out of the room because it was taking away from me focusing on them.

"Is there any explanation for it?" Helen

asked. She didn't seem upset, but it didn't really mean anything.

I knew that I probably could have thrown Stella under the bus but honestly, it wasn't my style to do so. She'd definitely been the cause of my mistake, but it wouldn't do me any good to tell anyone else that.

"I first want to sincerely apologize for this. I am normally on top of my game and I don't want to downplay this. I'm glad that this was caught before the patient had real conse- quences," I began. "I believe that it is my fault. I've been working a lot lately and I think I might just be tired."

Helen smiled at me. "I believe that to be the case," she agreed.

I couldn't hide the shocked expression on my face. "You do?"

"Kallie, I've been doing this for a long time. Before you came into this office I'd already checked your record and your schedule, not to mention all the good things that I've heard about you. I am going to make a note of this in your file and I will be recommending to your attending that you scale your hours back some. We're sending you home early today and we'll make a note of this in your file. If something else happens, there will be more serious consequences," she explained.

"I understand, and it won't happen again," I smiled at her. I felt like a weight had been lifted off of me.

Helen had me sign some papers and told me to be on my way. She also let me know that I wouldn't be treating the patient anymore and that they'd have a nurse assist me with my tests for a while. It was a little hand holding, but I couldn't complain, since the alternatives might have been worse.

I left the office soon after and headed downstairs to grab my stuff. After I had my purse, I was about to head out, but I decided to see if I could find Stella. I walked the hall and popped my head into a couple of rooms before I spotted her. She was just coming out of a patient room. I called out to her and she stopped.

"Did you need something?" Stella asked with ice in her voice.

"Only to say something to you," I replied. "I just got called up to Human Resources. It seems that I made a mistake with a test."

"You're my resident, but the test results are on you," she said.

"Be that as it may, when they asked me about what happened, I suddenly remembered that it was your unprofessional outburst that took my mind off of the tests and made me mess up." I was making sure to keep my voice down since no one else needed to know my business. Stella's eyes had gone wide. "Relax. I didn't tell them what happened. I just wanted to tell you about it before I headed home for the day."

"Thanks," Stella replied through gritted teeth. "Was there something else?"

"I just wanted to tell you so that you knew I was being a friend to you even though you haven't really been one to me these last few days," I explained. I wasn't even mad at the situation. I was more disappointed than anything.

"Kallie," Stella spoke and her tone had softened some, "I just wanna say I'm s—"

I held up my hand to stop her. "Save it. I don't need you to apologize cause I just did you a solid. I'm going home. We can talk some other time."

I knew it was rude to dismiss Stella but it

was in my best interest to get the hell out of the hospital as quickly as I could. I was being sent home for the day for the first time ever. I felt like I was back in high school getting sent home early for not wearing uniform.

I thought I was making it out without another situation but as my luck would have it, I spotted Christian coming out of a meeting. It looked like he was headed towards the same elevator that I was.

$\approx$

## Christian

I STOPPED WALKING when I spotted Kallie. I had just finished up an important conference call when I heard what could only be described as a heated discussion on the other side of the door. I'd recognized Kallie's voice immediately and from the way that it sounded, she was pissed off about something.

"Hello Dr. Jameson," I called out to her. She was walking towards me. I looked down at her thick legs in her black pants. It had been awhile since I'd spoken to her.

"Hello Christian," she answered robotically as she kept right on moving passed me without stopping. I hadn't run into her in a while either so I decided to use that chance to try and speak with her. I followed behind her until she reached the elevator and pressed the button.

"I haven't heard from you in a while," I said to her. She wasn't looking at me. In fact, she was staring intently at the button for the elevator like she was going to make it come faster. I cleared my throat a little and went on. "How is everything?"

"I can't do this right now." She leaned forward and pressed the down button on the elevator a few more times impatiently.

"Do what?" I asked. "Where are you going?" I looked down at my watch. I knew what time she'd come in that day because I asked around. It was too early for her to be taking a break.

"I'm going home for the day," she answered as the elevator finally arrived. A few people got off but thankfully we had it to ourselves. Kallie pressed the button for the basement, most likely heading towards the parking garage

"Why? Is everything alright?" She certainly didn't seem like everything was alright.

"Does it seem like it?" she snapped at me.

"Look, I don't know what's wrong with you but I'm here if you wanna talk," I held up my hands trying to show her I meant no harm. "Matter of fact, why don't we go out to dinner sometime and we can talk about what's going on with you?"

The elevator doors opened on the basement level and we both stepped out. Kallie was about to head through the last set of double doors before the garage but I put my hand on the door to stop her from opening it, forcing her to give me attention. She looked up at me with a blank look in her eyes.

"Did you hear me before? When can I come and pick you up?" I asked. Like most women, Kallie just needed some prodding in the right direction. I knew that she had an attitude with me from before because she felt I wasn't giving her enough attention but it wasn't my fault. I was busy a lot.

"You can't," she said flatly.

"Why not?"

"I'm seeing someone, Christian," Kallie

said. She took a deep breath and started to push on the door. "Can I go now?"

I didn't say another word as I took my hand off the door and let her pass. She disappeared, mostly likely headed towards her car. I made my way back to the elevator and to the floor that I'd just come from.

I hadn't meant to appear so shell-shocked in front of Kallie, but what she'd said had thrown me for a loop. I hadn't been expecting her to drop such a bomb on me. It hadn't even been that long since she and I'd stopped messing around and all of a sudden she was with someone else? Not to mention that she was even claiming whoever he was.

I felt my body grow hot with anger as I recalled the mysterious flowers that had arrived for her. I might have tried to pass them off as a gift from me but now that she'd revealed this relationship to me, it dawned on me that they were probably from whoever this new dude was.

I was a man on a mission as I made my way down the hall. I might have looked calm, cool, and collected on the outside but I was actually pissed off. I wanted to get more information but I knew I had to play it smart.

I knocked on the office door of the person who'd be able to help me out.

"Come in," a female voice said. I turned the knob and pushed the door open.

"Mr. Harper, what are you doing here?" Dr. Fraser looked up at me from behind her desk. She was doing something on her computer but focused her attention on me when I came in.

"Dr. Fraser...Stella, I was wondering if I might have a moment of your time," I said. She looked skeptical but motioned for me to sit.

"Is everything alright?" she asked.

"Well, and please let me know if I'm over-stepping my boundaries, but I wanted to ask you about Kallie...Dr. Jameson I mean. I know you two are close." I stammered out the words.

Stella and I weren't especially close but from what I knew of her she was incredibly smart. She could clearly see right through my little act, but she played along with it.

"What did you wanna know?" she asked as she leaned back in her chair.

"Well, I was on a call earlier and I heard her voice get kind of loud. I wanted to know if everything was alright between you two," I answered.

Stella folded her arms across her chest and if I didn't know any better, I'd assume that there was a slight smirk on her face. "Kallie has changed a lot since she started dating one of her former patients," she said.

"A former…" I couldn't even finish my statement. Everything clicked in my head and I felt even more pissed off than I had initially. I felt like Kallie was making a fool of me and no one did that. I realized then that I would have to step in. "Who is he?"

## CHAPTER 4

### Kallie

O n my way home from work I had to turn my music up to drown out my thoughts. I couldn't believe that I'd messed around and let myself get sent home. Granted, I knew that Stella could have taken a portion of the blame for distracting me but ultimately I should have never started doing the tests knowing that I was so distracted.

I didn't know what to do with myself since I'd planned on being at work all day. When I got in the house I cleaned everything up and then threw myself down onto the couch to watch some TV. I pulled out my phone and sent Miles a text message telling him to hit me up when he wasn't busy. I ended up drifting off to sleep but was awoken a while later to the sound of the phone vibrating with a message.

Miles and I struck up a conversation via text. I was trying to get him to call me but when he said he was busy, I ended up sending a series of texts explaining what had happened. He could probably tell by all the messages that he was getting that I was upset. He kept telling me that I needed to relax.

The conversation died down a little while later after Miles said he was busy and would hit me back when he got a chance. I got up and decided to take a long, hot shower. I lit some candles and let their scents fill the bathroom before I got in. It was exactly what I needed to help get the stress of the day off my mind.

After I got out I lotioned up and put on a pair of pajama shorts and a tank top. I was headed into the living room to find something on TV and figure out where I wanted to order my dinner from. No sooner than I'd sat down on the couch there was a knock at the door. I wasn't expecting any visitors and my doorman hadn't called up about anyone. I got up and cautiously walked towards the door.

"Who is it?" I called out from a few feet away. I was always cautious when it came to stuff like that.

"It's me," said a deep voice that instantly put a smile on my face. I felt my body release some tension as I headed to the door to unlock it.

Miles was standing there looking handsome. He was wearing a pair of light blue jeans that had rips in the front of them. He had on a white t-shirt that hugged his muscled, tattooed body.

"What are you doing here?" I asked, stepping aside to let him in and closing the door behind him. "And what's in those bags?"

Miles set the bags that he was carrying down on the kitchen counter. "I brought you some dinner and some of that wine we like," he said. "You seemed like you'd need it after the day you had. Did you eat?"

I shook my head. "No, I was actually about to order something, but this smells good. What'd you get?"

"I went to a steakhouse and picked us up some stuff. Two rib eyes and some baked potatoes and stuff. I've had it before. It tastes good," he explained.

I walked over in front of him and hopped up onto the counter, bringing my head closer to his. "Thank you for doing this," I said as I grabbed him by the shirt and pulled him closer to me, "I really appreciate it."

"It's nothin', baby. You know I'm always gonna look out for you," he proclaimed. Miles pecked me on the lips.

"Mmm," I cooed. "Do it again"

Miles started to plant soft, gentle kisses all over my face and neck. If not for the smell of the food hitting me nose, we probably would have gotten it on right then and there.

"Baby, let's eat," I pleaded as I gently pushed him off of me. "Come on before the food gets cold."

"We can heat it up," he breathed as he tried to lift up my tank top. I knew that if I let him get that far, it would be a wrap, so I kindly hopped off the counter.

Almost on cue, my stomach growled. "See, I'm hungry. You heard that monster roar?"

Miles chuckled. "Sounded like a full-blown dragon or some shit."

The food was as delicious as Miles said it would be. I was impressed, so impressed that I told him we should go there in person sometime soon. I immediately headed over to the couch after eating. We were halfway through the second bottle of the wine that Miles had brought and he was rubbing my feet while we watched a movie. For all of the stress that I'd been feeling earlier in the day, my evening had been just as relaxing.

I knew that leaving Miles hot and bothered earlier would come back to get me later on, not that I minded though. My legs and feet were strewn over his lap as we watched. The massage that he was giving me was slowly starting to creep up from my feet to my legs and then to my thighs.

I finally turned my head to look at him. I found the sneaky smirk he had on his face adorable.

"What?" he teased.

"You so nasty," I joked as I turned my attention back to the television screen.

Miles' big hands kept making their way up my body until they'd reached the bottom of the short shorts. His fingers ran across my bare thighs a few times before he slipped them up the shorts and closer towards my wet spot.

Slowly, be pushed his finger inside of me. I tried not to move as he did it. I was enjoying the little game we were playing. Miles' finger moved up until it was right on top of my clit. He pressed at it gently, sending a chill through my whole body. I couldn't help but to shift my legs a little then.

It went on like that for a few minutes. Miles would press at me like an instrument and I'd move my body or make noises. At a certain point he just kept moving his fingers in and out of me. I couldn't front anymore as I started to moan. I tried to grab at his hand to pull it away from me, but he wouldn't let me.

"Oh...oh Miles," I moaned passionately. I turned my body so that it was angled better on top of his. He put his other hand up my tank top and started to massage one of my breasts. My body shook and jerked with my orgasm. I bit my lip and looked at him with seduction in my eyes. It felt like my body was on fire.

I was moving like an animal as I rushed over to him. I grabbed at his shirt and pulled it over his head. Climbing on top of him to straddle him, I started to kiss him passionately. His little trick with his hands had gotten me into the mood for real.

Miles lifted himself and me off the couch just enough for him to pull off his pants and underwear. I felt his legs move under me as he kicked of his sneakers. He'd grabbed a condom from his jeans but I took it from him and slid it on his dick myself.

Once it was on, I stood briefly to take off my own clothes. I stood in front of him naked for a few seconds so he could admire me. He jerked his dick a few times while staring and then licked his lips, a signal for me to come back to him.

I straddled him again, this time slower. I eased my body down onto his and let him fill me up inch by inch. Miles began licking and sucking at one of my breasts while playing with the nipples of the other with his hands. I threw my head back in ecstasy as I started rocking my body back and forth on his.

I don't know what it was about the moment but there was so much passion in the way we made love to one another. It wasn't just that it was feeling great. We stared into one another's eyes throughout the entire thing. We kissed slowly and took time to touch and caress one another. We kept repeating how we felt about one another. It felt like something out of a dream.

After we finished and got cleaned up, we headed into my room. I wasn't too tired and neither was Miles, so we ended up putting a movie on. I drifted off to sleep after a while, only to be awoken in the middle of the night.

Miles' phone was vibrating like crazy next to the bed. I guessed he was knocked out because he hadn't made a move to answer it. I shook him a little bit to get him up.

Miles rolled over and groggily answered the phone. I could hear the sleep in his voice as he coughed to try and clear it up. I don't know what was being said to him on the other end of the phone, but it must've been some bad news.

"What?" Miles bolted out of the bed and into the living room. I could hear him moving around in the living room. I had a bad feeling in the pit of my stomach. I grabbed the sheet off the bed and wrapped it around my body before heading out into the living room. Miles was still talking on the phone as I sat down.

"What time does it leave?" he asked as he stuffed his foot into his sneaker. "Text me all the info. I'm not gonna remember that." He paused again while listening. "Alright, peace."

"What happened? Where are you going? It's the middle of the night," I said. I was obviously concerned about whatever was going on with him. Something serious had to have happened for him to jump and be ready to get on the move.

He stopped moving and sat back on the couch. He wasn't wearing a shirt, so I could see that he was breathing quickly. "I got a call from my connect. One of his people got hit."

"What does that have to do with you?" I asked.

"He got hit cause of the connect's loyalty to me. And to make it worse, the dude who got killed is one of my connects' cousins," he explained. I could see the troubled look on his face as he spoke to me.

"What are you gonna do?"

"I gotta meet with the connect. The only thing is that he's not in Chicago. I gotta go to meet him in New York. He has a plane to take me tomorrow night so I gotta get stuff ready here before I go." Miles' face was full of concern.

"Come back to bed," I responded. He looked surprised by what I said so I went on. "Miles, it's—" I looked down at the cable box for the time. "3:27 in the morning. There's nothing you can do right now. Everybody is sleeping. Besides, you don't wanna make any moves based on emotion and not logic. Just come back to bed and you can think it over in the morning to see how you wanna handle it."

Miles didn't say anything, but I could see that he was considering my words. He finally came to a decision and said he'd stay. We got up and headed back to the room. I snuggled up to him and drifted off to sleep.

The following morning, I got up before Miles did so that I could make breakfast. I knew that he'd probably be on his way as soon as he got up so I wanted to have it ready for him. I whipped up some bacon and eggs with grits and toast. I happened to have some orange juice so I poured us out some of that as well.

He was pleasantly surprised when he came out to find the meal on the table. He sat down to eat while I finished up the dishes before heading to my plate.

"So I was thinking it would be nice if you came with me to New York," Miles said. The words caught me off guard. My back was to him but I turned around to make sure that I'd heard him correctly.

"What?"

"New York," he repeated. "It would be cool if you were able to come with me. I know I'm going for work but it could be a nice little getaway for us after I handle my business."

I walked over to him and sat down at the table across from where he was. "Are you serious?" I asked.

He nodded. "Yeah, why wouldn't I be?" He tilted his head to the side. "So, what you think?"

I didn't even have to think about the answer that I wanted to give him. "I would love to, but I can't. Not with everything that happened at work. I don't know if I'd be able to take a day or two off at such short notice and then with me getting sent home early, it does add on to it too."

He only looked a little disappointed. "Damn, alright. You don't think they'll make an exception?"

I shrugged my shoulders. "Honestly, I don't know. You know how Stella has been acting lately and I don't even wanna put that on her. It could go left and I don't need another incident with human resources."

Miles nodded with understanding. "I feel you. Well, I shouldn't be gone too long, so it won't be too bad."

"That's true. And you know that if I can find a way to get off, I'm on the first thing smoking straight to New York," I said with a smile. "I just want you to be careful.'

"I'm always careful," he responded.

I shook my head. "Miles, I'm being serious. I want you to be safe when you're out there."

"I will. You got nothin' to worry about," he assured me. "You just try and get a day off so you can keep me out of trouble."

"I'll try my hardest," I said.

I dropped my head a little bit. I was thinking about the potential dangers that he could be facing in New York and it got me a little upset. I knew that Miles was always careful, but it wouldn't do anything to make me feel better. I always just felt like he was safest around me but maybe that was just my own feelings. If I could see him, I knew he was safe and not in danger somewhere.

Miles must have noticed the upset look on my face. He got up to comfort me. Leaning down over the back of my chair, he wrapped his arms around me and hugged me tightly. He kissed me gently on the neck. I could smell the scent of his cologne lingering on his clothes.

"I'm serious," he said. "I'm gonna be as careful as possible. Just don't sit around stressing yourself out over it. I'm gonna be fine."

I didn't even get a chance to eat my food. The comfort that Miles was giving me soon turned into love making. I hadn't planned on it, but those soft kisses that he was planting on my neck and face had gotten me all hot and bothered. When he reminded me that he was leaving later in the evening and we wouldn't have the chance to have sex for a while, I gave in. We ended up doing it right there on the counter.

When it was finally time for Miles to leave, I ended up driving him to the air strip. I'd never seen a private plane before, so I didn't know where they left from. The connect that Miles was working with must have been a big shot because it seemed like no expense had been spared.

It was dark when we arrived but it seemed like everyone there had been waiting on Miles. They greeted him by name and went over his itinerary. Since it wasn't a regular airport they didn't have a regular security system. I got to go with Miles all the way to the jet that he was taking. He showed me on board and I had to admit that I was impressed.

I'd seen private planes and things like that on television before but actually being on board one was something entirely different. It was bigger than I'd expected it to be. Miles was the only passenger so he had the entire thing to himself, save for a small crew of people. The flight from Chicago to New York wasn't a long one but it seemed like he'd be comfortable the entire time he was in the air.

"Miles, promise me that you'll be careful," I said. We'd gone back inside the main building as I was about to head back home and let him be on his way. I was feeling emotional about the time we'd be apart, but I knew it was something he needed to do.

"I promise," he said as he kissed me on the lips. "I promise."

"Call me when you land," I said. "I know you'll be busy but try and keep in contact."

"I got you," he assured me. "You got nothing to worry about."

## CHAPTER 5

Getting sent home early had really pissed me off. But I was glad for it after a while because it was a nice break. I'd been doing overtime like crazy without even meaning to, so it felt good to have those few extra hours to myself.

When I went into work for my next shift I was feeling better about a lot of things. I made it a point to stop in the Human Resources office and speak to Helen. I apologize again for the situation and made it clear that I wouldn't let something like that happen again. I'd already spoken to her about the situation but I wanted her to know how committed I was. It was important for me to maintain a

good reputation with people, especially admin-
istration

I check in with Stella, who was still freezing
me out. I didn't sweat it though. She gave me a
rundown on who I'd be working with for the
day and told me about a patient who'd ended
up getting better overnight.

The first patient that I needed to check in
with was Anthony Miller. He was a 32-year-old
diabetic who'd been having issues with a
medication that someone else had prescribed to
him. He'd been complaining of dizziness and
fatigue and when he came into the emergency
room, his blood pressure was sky high. We
admitted him and had him for a couple of days.

I was walking down the hall towards his
room when I was pulled into an empty patient
room. It happened so fast that I didn't know
whether to scream or try and run. When I
turned around to see who'd grabbed me, I was
surprised to see Christian standing there.

He wasted no time. He closed the door and
took a step towards me. His tall frame was
trying to lean down and kiss me while his hand-
held me by the arm. I quickly raised my hand
and pushed him away.

"What the hell is wrong with you?" I fumed. I couldn't believe that he'd literally pulled me into a room to try and pull that bullshit. "Don't grab on me, Christian."

He didn't seem fazed by my words at all. His eyes narrowed as he stared at me. "So I guess it's true then," he spat.

"What are you talking about?" I asked. He was acting funny and I didn't have the time. I wanted to get started on my rounds. I'd literally just told HR that I would be on top of things and I didn't want to make a liar out of myself.

"You're pushing me away, so you must really have a new man," he muttered. "Did you really let that dude replace me?"

I couldn't believe what I was hearing. Christian sounded like a child, not a grown ass man. "This has nothing to do with anyone else but me and you. I've already made it clear to you before how I feel about the way you treat me."

"So you just move on to one of your patients?" He had a smug look on his face as he dropped that bomb. I didn't know where he was getting his information from but he was apparently well-informed.

"How do you know that?" I asked. It wasn't

a direct confirmation but I had to have the assumption that Christian already knew more than he was letting on.

He shook his head at me. "Damn, you're not even gonna try and deny it."

I folded my arms across my chest. "Look, I don't know who you've been talking to but it wouldn't look too good on you if you've been going through hospital records. I can't believe you'd stoop so low."

Christian rolled his eyes. "I wouldn't compromise myself like that. Besides, a simple online search told me everything I needed to know about Miles. Do you know that he's a criminal?" He puffed his chest up. "What is it about this clown that turns you on? Is it the thrill? Do you have thing for bad boys? I wanna understand it."

The fact that Christian knew so much about Miles had definitely caught me off guard. I knew one thing for sure: I wasn't about to stand there and give him any answers. Without another word I pushed passed him and opened the door, leaving him standing there. I took a deep breath to gather my thoughts and continued down the hall towards my patient's room.

After I was done dealing with Mr. Miller, I headed back to the nurses' station on the floor. I'd left my cell phone there to charge. When I grabbed it, I got excited because I had a text message from Miles. I opened it up quickly and read through it.

*Wassup babe? Hope your day is going smooth. Something happened so shit went kind of left. I just can't wait to get back to you. I'll call you later when I get back to my hotel. Love you.*

I felt my stomach sink a little bit. I hated when people brought something up without going into detail. Why would he just mention that "something happened" instead of being more direct about it? My mind went to all sorts of places. He didn't say anything happened to him and I hoped it stayed that way.

I hoped more than ever that I'd be able to find a way to get some time off to go to New York. I wished that I could get someone to cover for me but as far as I knew no one was available. I was also sure that I couldn't count on Stella to do me any favors so I was on my own.

The next two days were a lot for me. I spoke

to Miles a handful of times, mostly at the end of the night or early mornings. It was easier for him to talk to me when he was alone in his hotel room so that was when we talked.

I was still worried about him but speaking to him helped to make it easier for me. I knew that there was nothing I could do since I wasn't with him. It would have helped me feel better though. Miles was only supposed to be gone for a day or two, but he told me that he had to stay a little longer.

According to him, his connect didn't seem to trust him after losing one of his men. He was putting in extra time to make sure that their relationship didn't get any worse. Miles said that he was going to find out exactly who the shooter was in exchange for the support of the connect. I enjoyed the fact that he'd become a lot more willing to speak to me about his other life. All I could do was keep warning him to be careful.

I was finishing up a double shift which would hopefully be my last one for a while when I was approached by Ashley. I'd just come out of a patient's room and was heading towards the elevator when she called out to me.

"Kallie, do you have a minute? I need a

favor," she said. Ashley and I had definitely become cool. I wouldn't say that we were close or anything like that, but we'd at least reached a level where we could be friendly with one another.

"What is it?" I asked.

"So, I have to go away in a couple of weeks. One of my cousins is having a baby shower out of town and I wanna go and surprise her," she began. "Would you be able to cover for me? It's just a day or two, nothing crazy."

Ashley didn't know it but she was the answer to my prayers in that moment. "What's in it for me?"

"I can cover for you this week or next if that's better," she replied.

I almost jumped for joy. "Yes! Would you be willing to do the rest of this week? I'm off so it wouldn't be too many."

Ashley nodded her head. "Yeah, no problem. I'll get the papers so we can make it official."

"You don't know how much of a lifesaver you are." I couldn't help but to smile. I would be able to see Miles.

The rest of my shift went by in a breeze. I

was feeling amped up about being able to fly to New York. I'd never been before so I was planning on making the most out of the trip.

When I left, I almost sped home. I needed to pack so I could go see my man.

## CHAPTER 6

As bothered as I could be by the security that Miles had following me around, they also came in kind of handy sometimes. I knew that normally I wasn't supposed to approach them but since I was heading out of the state, I thought it would be best to tell them. They were really helpful with getting everything planned out. They even drove me to the airport and I let them know not to tell Miles because it was a surprise.

The security thing was still in effect when I landed in New York. Some of Miles' guys came to pick me up once I arrived. As we drove through the streets of New York I felt like a tourist. I rolled my window down so I could properly see the sites as we drove by them. The city was alive. There were so many people, each of them wrapped up in their own worlds. I wondered where Miles was.

I got to the hotel and his security let me know that Miles wasn't there but he'd be back later on. It was perfect for me because I wanted to do something special for him.

I stepped into the large room and looked around. It was similar to the room that Miles and I stayed in when we went to Miami but not as big. There was a large living room area with a nice bar and a huge TV on a mantle. The room was decorated in blue and white, giving it a calming feeling. I headed into the bedroom and saw that there were two beds. Miles' suitcases were open on one with his clothes randomly lying around. The other bed was perfectly made.

I dropped my bag down on the floor and went to work. The head of the security detail told me that they were expecting Miles back within an hour or so, so I needed to move quickly. On the way to the hotel I had security stop at a florist shop. I picked up a couple of roses and sprinkled a trail of rose petals all around the bedroom leading up to the bed. I also had room service send up a bottle of champagne. The last part of the seduction was in my bag.

I brought along some sexy lingerie that I wanted Miles to see me in. I changed out of my outfit from earlier and put on the bra and panties set. The white lace looked good against my pecan colored skin.

I checked myself out in the mirror and turned around right on time. I was stationed in the bedroom, but I could hear the electronic buzz of the door's lock opening. My phone was next to me and it lit up. Miles was calling me as he came back. I couldn't help but to feel warm and smile. He'd finally gotten some alone time and the first thing he wanted to do was talk to me.

My phone lit up again as Miles called. He still hadn't made it into the bedroom, but I could hear the clanging of glasses in the living room. He must have been pouring himself a drink. My phone was still buzzing as Miles' footsteps got closer to the room.

"Oh shit," Miles almost jumped when he saw me. The glass that he was holding in his hand almost slipped out. "You're one amazing woman."

Miles put his drink down on the table by the door. I was sitting on the bed that was farthest from the door but he made it over to me in two big steps. He was standing in front of me staring at my body in the lingerie. I scooted back on the bed a little bit more to give him a better view. I had seduction in my eyes as I stared up at him.

He was on me like an animal. Miles wasted no time pulling his shirt over his head and kneeling down in front of me. It felt like he was hungry for me. His mouth and tongue licked and kissed all over my stomach and lower.

Miles pulled at my panties as he propped my legs up on his shoulders. He started to lick at my inner thighs, sending tingling waves through my body. I put my hand on the back of his head as he started eating away at me. He didn't even take my panties off, only pulling them to the side enough for his tongue to get inside of me.

"How'd you get here?" Miles breathlessly asked. He'd pulled himself out from between my legs long enough to get the question out before burying himself again.

"I...." I couldn't say anything because I started moaning. I threw my head back in ecstasy. "Ashley and I... ooh," I moaned loudly. Miles I couldn't finish a sentence. Every time I tried to I'd feel my body get warm. It was feeling too good.

I pulled Miles' head back a little bit so he could look at me. "I want the real thing," I cooed. I was staring him in the eyes letting him know just how badly I wanted it.

Miles didn't say anything. He got up off the floor and kicked off his sneakers. His dick was rock hard already when he dropped his underwear. I knew that it had only been a few days since we'd seen one another but I felt like it was longer. I missed him and wanted him to know it. I kicked off my panties and threw let them fall to the floor. Laying on my back, I raised my legs and spread them wide open, giving him a full view of everything.

Miles propped my legs up on his shoulders and slowly eased himself inside of me. He paused for a moment and then went to work. His hips rocked back and forth as he moved himself in and out of my body. He motioned for me to take my bra of and watched as my breasts bounced with every stroke.

We went at it for what felt like forever. The two of us were in sync and moved like we were one. We didn't have to say anything when we wanted to change positions. It just happened naturally.

I was on the verge of my third orgasm when Miles grunted in my ear that he was close to his own climax. I was propped up on my knees on the bed but sitting straight up. My back and ass were pressed against his body. I was glad that the air conditioning was on, otherwise I know we would have been sweating up a storm.

"Fuck!" Miles cried out loudly. His hands had a firm grip on my waist as he pulled me back onto him a few more times before the two of us collapsed on the bed. He eased himself out of me and laid there for a few seconds to catch his breath. I'd gotten a full night's sleep, but I felt ready for a nap.

Miles and I got ourselves cleaned up and climbed into the bed together. It was the middle of the day but with the curtains drawn it felt like night time. The cool air from the AC was filling the room and made me snuggle up to him. I inhaled deeply, taking in his scent as I did.

"Yo, you know you shocked the shit out of me by showing up here right?" Miles said with a chuckle. "You're something else."

"It worked out because Ashley wants a day off in a few weeks, so she asked me to trade with her," I explained. "So now I'm yours for a few more days."

"I was planning on coming back home tomorrow, but since you're here I can get another day or two." Miles had a grin on his face. I knew that my showing up hadn't been expected but he seemed to be enjoying it.

"How'd everything go with your connect?" I asked. It had been on my mind for a while so I figured it would be the perfect time to ask.

Miles sighed. "He's a hardhead but it worked out, or at least it will. I just need to handle the source of the problem and every-thing'll be fine," he explained.

"I'm sure you'll take care of it," I replied. I leaned in and pecked him on the lips.

"Definitely," he said. "But I'm apologizing now cause when we get back, I'm in grind mode. You're probably not gonna see too much of me."

I nodded my head in understanding. He was serious about his work so I knew that he was going to want to take care of this as soon as he could.

"Well, we're here now so let's just worry about that." I got up and wrapped the sheet from the bed around my body. I walked over to the curtains and pulled the stick that opened them, letting the bright lights of the day into the room.

The late afternoon sun was only just starting to move towards setting. I looked out at the tall buildings and down to the street below. There were so many people moving around without a care in the world. I understood in that moment what people saw in New York and why so many people moved their despite it being so expensive. It just seemed to have a certain magic to it.

"What do you want to do for the rest of the day?" I asked Miles as I turned back to face him. I took a moment to admire him. His peanut butter colored skin and tattoos made him look like some kind of model with the way the sunlight was hitting him. He turned his body towards me and I couldn't help but to look down the bulge in the front of his boxer briefs. Even when he wasn't hard it was apparent that he was packing.

"We could get food later," he said. "You've never been here right?"

I shook my head. "I've always wanted to come but never got around to it."

"Well we're only here for a little bit but we can make the most of it. We can find somewhere to eat at. We could get fancy down here or head uptown and get some soul food."

"I'm with whatever you want," I said.

"Nah, you choose," he replied with a shake of his head. "It's whatever you wanna do today."

I walked back over to the bed and climbed on top of him. "Well, I hope you brought some good sneakers with you cause I wanna be a tourist."

He playfully rolled his eyes. "Oh God. Empire State Building and all that?"

"Whatever we can get to," I winked at him.

Miles and I somehow managed to get ourselves out of bed. We almost ended up having sex again, but I told him that I really wanted to get out and see the city. We showered and got dressed.

Miles had a list of places that he said we should see. I was a little corny, so I wanted to ride on the top of one of those double decker tour busses. He wasn't with it but he did have his security drive us all around and he pointed places out. We hit up all of the places that I only heard about. We walked through Central Park and Times Square. We headed uptown to Harlem and I saw the historic neighborhood. It looked like a place I could live one day.

Miles and I headed all the way downtown to the Meatpacking District. He'd gotten us a reservation at a fancy rooftop steakhouse. It was beautifully decorated and had an amazing view of the Hudson River.

"Babe, this place is so nice," I gushed. We were seated and sipping our wine while we waited for the food to arrive. "You know I love a good steak."

"And this place has the best. I looked it up online," he said. He took a deep breath. "So, I wanted to give you something. I wasn't gonna give it to you until I got back but since you popped up I decided to give it to you now." He reached into the pocket of his pants and pulled out a small box before handing it to me.

"You don't have to get me gifts," I said. He knew that I had my own money but he always wanted to take care of me.

"You better take this gift and stop playing," he joked as he pushed it further towards me.

I reached out and took it from him. Opening the small box, I found a diamond tennis bracelet. "Miles this is gorgeous!"

"Only the best for you," he smiled. He reached out and helped me snap it on my wrist.

"I love it. I promise to never take it off." I looked down at my new bracelet with admiration in my eyes.

"I'm glad you like it. I just wanted to get you something special," Miles smiled at me.

We enjoyed the rest of our dinner and when we were done Miles took us back up to the Central Park area. He planned for us to do one of those romantic horse and carriage rides through the park. I was excited about it at first because I'd always seen stuff like that on TV. Reality was much different though. I took one look at the skinny horse and then smelled the odor coming off of it before I told Miles we could just head back to the hotel. We ended up laughing about it the entire way there.

The next morning Miles was up early. He said that he had a meeting to go to, but he'd see me later on around lunch time. He encouraged me to go shopping and left a stack of money by the bed for me to do it with. Shopping was one thing that had been at the top of my list. Stella had been to New York before and told me all about how it was the best shopping experience she'd ever had.

I was excited as I took my shower and got dressed. I told Miles' security where I was headed and I also let them know they could drop me off and pick me up but I'd be fine to walk alone. The chances of anyone trying anything on such a busy street as Fifth Avenue were slim to none.

As I made my way from store to store I couldn't help but to think about how much things had changed since I'd gotten with Miles. I was on a last-minute trip to New York City, shopping on the world famous Fifth Avenue. It wasn't as though I couldn't have done any of this before, but Miles had definitely brought some much-needed excitement into my world.

If it wasn't for him, my life would probably still consist of gym, home, and work.

I got back to the hotel awhile later. Miles was already inside the room. He was sitting on the couch watching a basketball game when I walked in.

"Damn, did you leave anything in the stores?" He couldn't help but to laugh as he looked down at all the different bags in my hands.

"Oh please," I smirked. "It's not that much. Besides, it's not even all for me. I got you some sneakers and some shirts."

"You didn't have to do that," he said.

"I would have felt bad spending all that money you left on me," I responded.

"That's why I like you. You don't only think about yourself. That's a good quality." Miles got up and took the bags out of my hand, taking them into the bedroom and placing them on the bed. I followed him into the room.

"How'd your meeting go?" I asked him. I loved the fact that we always asked about each other's day.

"It was cool. Can't get better till I get back

and handle these clowns. We don't have to talk about that though."

Miles and I ended up spending two more days in New York. Since he was done with his business stuff I had him all to myself and I wanted to take advantage. We hit up every neighborhood that I'd heard about from other people. We continued sightseeing and went out to eat at different places whenever we got hungry. I enjoyed how normal the whole thing felt.

Our last day had finally arrived. Miles had just checked out of the hotel room and we were in his car about to head to the airstrip where the jet was waiting for us. I was happy that I'd finally get a chance to ride on it as opposed to just seeing it.

It felt like a familiar scene on the way there. We were still about twenty minutes away from where the plane was when we heard sirens behind us. I looked down to see if Miles was speeding but it looked like everything was alright. He just shrugged his shoulders and pulled over. He grabbed for his license and registration.

The cops had pulled Miles and I over once

before and it terrified me. I wasn't used to dealing with the police so to have them come and snatch Miles right out of the car had been a lot for me. This time around I felt better prepared. I wasn't anywhere close to nervous as they got out of their car and made their way to ours.

The cops were assholes. They asked us where we were going and didn't offer up any explanations for why they'd pulled us over. Miles handed them his license and registration and when they came back to the car they asked both of us to step out.

The police weren't offering up and answers as they looked through the car. It was a rental so there was nothing inside of it except for our water bottles and bags. I didn't know what it was that they hoped to find but when they found nothing, they let us go.

We pulled off and continued on our way to the airstrip.

"I'm sorry about that," Miles said. "You know how these pigs can be."

"It's fine," I assured him. "I wasn't scared, not like last time. It's kind of normal now."

Miles shook his head. "Don't say that."

"Say what?"

"That this is normal for you," he answered.

I couldn't figure out why he seemed so annoyed. "I'm just saying that wasn't the first time and it probably won't be the last. It's just something I gotta get used to."

Miles sucked his teeth but didn't say anything for a while. I could tell he was thinking hard about something. He was gripping the steering wheel tightly and his eyes were super focused on the road.

"Are you alright?" I asked him after a few minutes of awkward silence.

"Yeah...yeah I'm cool. I was just thinking about a choice I gotta make."

"What would that be?" I pressed him.

"You'll find out soon enough. But just know that I don't want this for you," he explained. "None of this shit should be normal to you."

"Miles, it's fine. We don't have to make it a big thing," I shot back. I could see that what I'd said before had really affected him.

"It's cool. I'm gonna handle it," he said mysteriously. I didn't know what it was that he'd been thinking about but from the way he was speaking, I could tell it would end up affecting the both of us. I just hoped that he didn't do anything to jeopardize anyone. Christian was arrogant and pompous, but he was also a blowhard. He would never try to force himself on me for real.

CHAPTER 7

Spending all those days in New York with Miles had been fun. But as it usually happens, life gets in the way and those things must end. We landed back in Chicago early one morning. I was returning to work that day so Christian decided to drop off at work. He'd have someone drop my luggage and stuff off back at my house.

Miles pulled up outside of the hospital. I looked at the tall gray building through the car window and couldn't say that I'd missed it too much. Miles hopped out of the car and came around to my side to open the door. He could be a real romantic like that sometimes.

"You got everything you had with you?" he asked as he grabbed my hand helping me step out of the car.

I nodded my head. "Yeah."

Miles put his arm around my waist and leaned down to kiss me. Now that we were back in Chicago I knew that he'd be busy. He told me that he needed to finish up stuff for his connect so I knew it might be some time before I saw him again. All of those emotions were passed along to me in the kiss he planted on me.

"Kallie," a deep voice called out to me. I broke the kiss with Miles and turned my head to see Christian walking towards us. He must have been there for a meeting or something since he was dressed in a nice, form fitting, blue suit. "Good Morning.

"What the fuck does he want?" I grumbled to myself under my breath, low enough for only me to hear it. I was hoping that he might just go one about his day, but he didn't. He made it a point to make his presence known until he was acknowledged. "Good morning Christian."

Christian stood there awkwardly for a few seconds with a smug look on his face. When it became apparent that I wasn't about to make any introductions, he took it upon himself to do so. He extended his hand in Miles' direction.

"Hello. I'm Christian. You must be a *friend* of Kallie's," Christian said. He still had that same stupid grin plastered all over his face.

I looked at Miles, who'd only just taken Christian's hand and shook it. I could see from the look on his face that he remembered Christian from his time in the hospital. Judging by their handshake, it looked like they were trying to squeeze the life out of one another's hands.

"I'm Miles," he introduced himself. "Nice to meet some of Kallie's coworkers."

Christian laughed in such a phony way. "Oh no, I'm not a coworker. I don't have the time to get my elbows dirty like everyone else. I *am* a Board Member though."

I rolled my eyes. Christian had some nerve making it seem like he was so much better than I was. I was a doctor and he was a trust fund baby who'd just so happened to be lucky in business. The conversation had only been happening for less than a minute and already I felt like it was too long and needed to end.

"Well Christian, Miles was just about to be off, so if you'll excuse us," I interrupted. I didn't need him hanging around any longer than necessary.

"No problem. I wouldn't want to interrupt." Christian's eyes scanned my whole body quickly before he left without another word to me or Miles.

Once Christian walked into the building Miles turned back to me. The expression on his face was a serious one. "I remember that clown. That's the nigga you were dating before right?"

I nodded my head. "Yeah, but it's in the past now. I told him we're together so it's not a big deal."

Miles shook his head. "Nah, there's something about him I don't like. If that nigga comes near you or tries something, you need to let me know, cool?"

I averted Miles' gaze for just a few seconds too long, letting him know something was up. I'd had that little run in with Christian the other day when he pulled me into the patient room and tried to kiss me. It was a little on the rough side but I handled it. I wasn't about to let Miles know that though. Who knew what he would do to Christian if he found out?

"Kallie, did something happen? That nigga do something to you?" He was searching my face for an answer and when I didn't say anything he got it. Miles tried to turn around and march into the hospital following Christian, but I firmly held onto his hand and pulled him back.

"Miles! Calm down. Don't do anything stupid," I warned. "It was nothing. I took care of it."

"I don't want him around you," he fumed. "Just let me go talk to him. That's all I wanna do."

I shook my head. "Let it go," I pressed him. "It's not even worth it. You already got other things on your plate. Christian ain't dumb. He knows not to mess with me."

Miles did a deep sigh and shook his head. "Call me if you need me. I can be here as soon as possible."

"I will," I said. I pulled his head down to me so I could kiss him again. "I'll see you later. I love you."

"Love you too," he said. He climbed back

into his car soon after we broke the kiss. He waited until he watched me disappear into the building before he finally pulled off.

All throughout the work day I was lucky enough to avoid Christian. I thought for sure that he'd come and find me at some point and would have something to say about Miles but he didn't. The day actually went pretty smooth. Stella stayed the hell out of my way and didn't ask me any questions about where I'd been for the last few days.

When I left work that night I had a craving for a nice salad. New York had been good to me and the food was amazing, but I'd really let myself eat everything in sight. I didn't want to gain any weight, so I stopped at the grocery store to pick up a couple of healthier food items.

I was walking towards the sliding double doors of the store when I noticed something. I'd parked pretty much right in front of the door but I could see two guys close to my car. I didn't recognize them as any of the security that Miles usually had follow me around. I was cautious as I stepped of the store. One of the men was white and the other appeared to be Spanish or

Middle Eastern. They were dressed in non-descript clothes.

I looked across the street and saw the doors open on the black truck that I'd become familiar with following me around. Miles' security hopped out and two of them were making their way towards me. However, they hung back as the two guys approached me and flashed badges.

"Hello ma'am. My name is Detective Thomas and this is my partner, Detective Singh," the white guy introduced himself. I stopped walking and didn't say anything so he went on. "Is your name Kallie Jameson?"

"Why?" I snapped. I wasn't used to the police approaching me. I'd had two other inter-actions with them, but they were both in the presence of Miles who I always assumed was their real target.

"Ma'am, this could go a lot easier if you'd corporate. You're not in any trouble. We're just trying to get to the bottom of things," Detective Thomas explained.

I hated when people asked questions they already knew the answer to. The clearly knew who I was and might have been following me around since they were looking at my car earlier. I knew that I needed to play it cool. Miles and I had spoken before about what to do if I ever found myself in a situation like this.

"I'm Kallie Jameson, but I'm sure you guys already knew that. What's all this about? I'm trying to get home," I asked.

"Ms. Jameson, are you—" Detective Singh started to speak but I cut him off.

"Doctor," I interjected.

He had a confused look on his face. "What?"

"It's not Ms. Jameson, its. Doctor Jameson. It's a title, not an option," I mouthed off. I knew that I was being a little difficult, but Miles made it clear that cops worked in tandem with one another. They would play off of one another and build up a momentum. He explained the easiest way to throw them off was to keep them from hammering questions.

Detective Singh rolled his eyes. "Sorry, *Dr. Jameson*, but are you acquainted with Miles Wilson?"

"We're close," I said. They waited for an explanation that wasn't coming. I wasn't about to give them anything to try and use against me.

I couldn't lie and say he was a patient. They'd be able to check that out in my records.

"Well Dr. Jameson, we only have a couple more questions for you if you don't mind," Thomas went on. "Do you know anything about what Mr. Wilson does for a living?"

I shook my head. "I don't ask questions."

Singh sighed and cut his eyes at his partner. They didn't say anything, but their look said it all. "So you guys are close but you don't know what he does for a living or how he pays for things?"

"I'm a doctor. I make my own money. I don't need anyone to pay for anything for me so no, I don't ask," I explained. The two of them exchanged another glance and chuckled to one another.

"Am I being detained or am I free to go?" I pressed them.

Singh walked closer to me and pulled something from his pocket. "Here's my card. You can give me a call in case you find out anything. But no, you're not being detained."

"There's nothing to find out," I said as I brushed past him towards my car. I didn't bother taking the business card from him.

I might have been putting on a brave show for the benefit of the police but inside I was shook. The cops stood there and watched me pull off. I didn't drive straight back to my house. I was feeling the paranoia creeping up on me so I took a roundabout way home with bunch of extra twists and turns. I was nervous and wanted to give Miles a call but I'd watched enough TV and spoken to him enough to know that would be the stupidest thing I could do. It would be alike an admission of guilt.

I didn't hear from Miles that night and I hadn't expected to. The security people had seen the whole thing go down. They didn't approach me afterwards, but I was sure that they'd contacted Miles and told him all about it.

I laid in bed that night wondering where he was and what he was doing. I wished he could come by because it would help me sleep better but it wasn't best for the situation. I thumbed at the beautiful bracelet that he'd given me as a sign of our love and wished he was there with me instead. I never took it off like I promised him.

Tossing and turning was all I did for the first hour of trying to get to sleep. I'd told Miles in

New York that things with the police were becoming normal but in reality they weren't. This new thing with them showing up places that I was had shaken me. In my head I couldn't help but to feel that this was turning into too much to deal with.

Miles had been laying low for a couple of days. I didn't even hear from him. Then, one night out of the blue a member of his security came knocking at my door. He said that Miles wanted to meet with me and gave me some time to get ready. I went with him and we drove out to a hotel in the suburbs of Chicago. He gave me a key and told me which room to head up to.

"Damn, I've missed you," Miles greeted me. I'd just walked into the room where he was and he was sitting on the bed. He looked up at me and smiled as I closed the door behind me. He looked more tired than I'd ever seen him.

"Are you alright?" I asked as I wrapped my arms around him and held him tightly. He took a deep breath and we didn't say anything for a while as we stayed wrapped up in each other.

"I'm good. How are you?" he asked as he

finally broke the hug. "I know it's probably been a rough couple of days."

I nodded. "Yeah, but it's nothing I can't handle."

Miles' mood got darker. "I can't believe those fucking pigs had the nerve to approach you."

"It was nothing," I assured him. "They just asked if I knew you and I gave them the usual answers that we'd talked about."

He shook his head. "Nah, they're taking this shit too far. They've got cops on their payroll too so they're trying to fuck with me by sending 'em after me. That's why I've been laying low."

"Are you close to handling things?" I asked.

"Yeah, but I want everything done sooner rather than later," Miles said with a sigh. "I never wanted any of this for you."

"Baby it's not your—"

"Don't tell me it's not my fault," he interrupted. "If I would have never brought you into my world, none of this shit would be happening to you. I just hope that my plan works out and we can finally get the nigga that killed the connects cousin. Once that's done, it's just a matter of getting the other niggas. The connect is gonna put his foot on their necks and make sure that they don't get any more product."

I maneuvered him over to the bed and sat him down. I started massaging his shoulders, hoping to relieve some of the stress and tension he was feeling. "It's gonna be alright," I assured him.

"Yeah it will be. Cause after this I'm done," he said.

"What do you mean?"

"I'm getting out of the game after this. I just need to settle this shit and then I can move on," he explained.

I stopped massaging him and moved around him so I could look him in the eyes. "Are you serious? You're really getting out?"

He nodded his head. "Yeah. I'd been thinking about it for a while but with all the stuff that's recently happened, I know it's time for it."

"I just want you to be safe," I said. "I've seen a lot of people try and get out and it didn't go so well for a lot of them."

"I'm careful. I'm always careful. I got good people around me too," he assured me.

Miles and I ended up staying at the hotel for

the night. It wasn't safe for him to come to mine and I never really went to his. All night long I couldn't stop thinking about his plan to get out of the game. I just hoped it worked out because it would mean that we could be together for real and not have to worry.

## CHAPTER 8

The cops paying me a visit had been a lot. It just added on to the stress that I'd already been feeling about Miles and I situation. It had sent me into a tailspin, but I'd recovered by spending time with Miles and reminding myself that he was careful. I didn't want to add on any more stress to his load by letting him know that I was worried. I just encouraged him to be safe and tried to go about my day as best I could.

Things must have been getting hot for him though. One night while I was at home watching the news, I saw a story about a drug dealer being killed. It felt like my soul almost left my body as I waited for them to tell the whole story. I was relieved when I found out that though it had been a high-ranking member of an organization, it had been from the gang that was opposing Miles'. I wondered to myself if that had been the person who'd murdered the connect.

I got my answer soon enough, at least in some form. I was at home making dinner when I heard a few loud knocks on my door. Miles' security was stationed around so they knew who my visitors were. I figured it either had to be Miles himself or a member of their team sending a message.

I got the shock of my life when I opened my door to find two detectives standing there. Unlike the dirty cops who'd found me outside the grocery store a few days ago, it was apparent from the beginning that they were police officers. I noted their oversized suits and the scent of their cigarettes filled the room.

The cops weren't taking no for an answer and asked to come inside. The two of them sat down with me for well over 20 minutes asking various questions. How did I know Miles? Were we dating? Did I know where he was? They made it apparent that they wanted to speak with him. I didn't give them any information. I couldn't. I honestly had no idea where he was or what he was doing so it made it easy to just tell them the truth. They left a business card with me and told me that it would be best if I called them if I'm contacted by him.

It had been a few days since I'd heard from Miles but he made sure to send word that he was fine through his security. They told me that Miles was laying low. They explained that he has to finalize things with the connect and then soon after that he would be fine. He apparently wanted to keep his distance from me until he'd gotten the connect's people under control. I knew he probably wanted to say that he loved or missed me but he couldn't send word of that through them.

As usual, I threw myself into my work in order to keep my mind off of things. Stella and I were still on ice but I didn't even really care anymore. I just focused on my patients as best I could and tried to keep my mind off of worry. I wished that my relationship with Miles could be a little bit more normal, but I knew what I'd signed up for.

It was a Thursday evening when I found myself at home catching up on TV. My day at work was long and tiring but thankfully it was over. I took a sip of the bottle of wine that I planned on finishing that night and spread some jam on a cracker. I found that when I was at home relaxing was best for me. Getting lost in a bottle of wine, some snacks, and a good show made it easier for me to not think about all the things I was worried about.

Three loud knocks came at my door. I jumped up on the couch and sat up to turn and look at the door. I checked my cell phone and saw that it was almost 10 o'clock at night. Who the hell could be at my door? Two more loud knocks came. I sat the glass of wine down and stood up to answer it. The only people who'd be rude enough to come to someone's house at this time of night could be the police. They'd also be the only ones that security would let up.

I had an attitude at that point. I flung the door open and rudely declared, "I haven't seen Miles!"

"Oh, the drug dealer hasn't been around?

Good thing." I was surprised to see Christian standing outside my door. I wondered how he'd gotten upstairs but then I realized that neither my doorman or security would have seen any reason to stop him. I made a mental note to let them all know that Christian wasn't allowed upstairs.

"What the hell are you doing here?" I asked. I had a firm grip on the door. I didn't want him to think he had any chances of getting inside my apartment.

"I hope that since you haven't seen him it means you've come to your senses about us," Christian said arrogantly. The look on his face was a serious one.

I rolled my eyes and scoffed. I made a move to start to close the door in his face but he wedged his foot in the door. I applied a little more pressure to try and get it out but he wasn't budging.

With little effort, Christian pushed the door open and I took a step back.

"You need to leave!" I demanded. I didn't know what was going on with him, but he needed to get it under control.

He took another step towards me. "I can't

believe you're really running around with a criminal." He stopped and shook his head. "You should be careful. If the people at the hospital found out it would ruin your reputation."

"Who I date *outside* the hospital has nothing do with my work when I'm there," I countered. I was getting more and more angry by the second. "And all the charges against him were dropped, if you must know."

"You think you've got everything figured out, don't you?" Before I could stop him, Christian leaned down and planted a kiss on my cheek. I quickly wiped it away.

"Goodnight," he said before he turned and walked out the door. I walked over to it and made sure to lock it.

I couldn't believe Christian had the audacity to come to my home at that time of night, acting the way that he was acting. I was a little afraid of what he might have done. My mind quickly moved to what might happen to him.

I knew that security would probably end up telling Miles about the visit and he would want details. I knew he wouldn't think I was cheating on him or something. I also didn't want to lie to him about what had happened with Christian but I knew that if I told him the truth, Miles would get angry and would want to go off. I couldn't let that happen. I would have to try and keep him as calm as possible after he found out.

## CHAPTER 9

"*Reunited and it feels so good,*" I sang out loud. I even did a little dance while doing it.

"You're crazy, you know that, right?" Miles responded. He was looking at me like I'd lost my mind. I kept on singing trying to get him to join me but he didn't.

The two of us were at my apartment. Though the last few days and weeks had been rough ones, it seemed like we could finally put a lot of that stuff behind us. Miles had shown up outside of my door one evening unannounced. He came in with flowers and apologies and explained to me that he could finally come back around for real. He explained most of what happened to me so that I could get the whole picture.

Miles' crew had been the main suspects in the murder of the opposing drug dealer. That was the reason that the cops had been on top of he and I the way that they had. However, Miles had another plan. He'd found out who murdered his connect's cousin and planted evidence on him that made it look like he was responsible for that and a lot more. The cops found the body and the evidence, and it was case closed.

"I'm just glad that we can hang out like normal people again," I cuddled up to him. The two of us were laying on my bed.

"Me too," he said as he pulled me closer and kissed me on the forehead. "I just hate that all this shit had to happen."

"I know," I tried to comfort him.

Miles shook his head. "Nah, you don't even know the half of it. Dude was crazy. I was gonna have to take him out at some point, even if he didn't mess with my connect. He was doing dumb shit; taking out civilians and shit like that. It just brings a whole lot of extra attention."

"You did what you felt you needed to do," I assured him. "That's all you could really do."

"Yeah, you're right," he said in agreement.

"Have you been looking for someone to take over for you? I remember from before you mentioned getting out of the game. Now that you don't have enemies, isn't it time?" I asked.

Miles took a deep breath. "Honestly, I haven't even thought too much about it. I've just been busy working on making things right in the streets. I haven't had time for much else. I've just been worried about making it back to you."

"I know."

Miles got silent for a moment and then sighed. He moved himself from underneath me and laid on his side so we could be face to face with one another. His body language said he was relaxed but there was a certain tension in his face that had me wondering what was on his mind.

"I definitely wanted to make sure that I came back to you since I heard that nigga Christian was here," Miles said. He didn't sound angry and his tone wasn't accusatory.

"Yeah, he was. I didn't invite him or anything like that. He just showed up one night.

I told security not to let him up anymore," I explained.

"It's cool. If I thought you'd cheated on me or something, I wouldn't be this calm," he said. "Why'd he come here though?"

"You gotta promise me you're gonna be calm," I pleaded.

Miles rolled his eyes and sat up in the bed. "Just tell me what happened."

"Not until you calm down," I said as I also sat up.

Miles took a forced deep breath. "I'm calm. Just tell me what happened."

I was hesitant to tell him but he already knew that Christian had showed up. There was no way that I could deny it. I didn't want to avoid the truth, but I wanted to find a way to soften the blow. When I realized there really wasn't one, I decided to just come clean about the whole thing.

"I thought he was the cops when he showed up," I began. "He came banging on the door and it was late so I assumed that's who it had to be. He showed up and I tried to get him to leave. Eventually he did."

Miles' eyes narrowed and he screwed his

face up at me. "What you mean eventually? What happened?"

I sighed. "Look, I kicked him out, that was the point. He tried to kiss me and stuff and he wouldn't let me close the door." Since I was being honest with him, I went on and explained what happened with Christian and I before when he'd pulled me into the patient room. I gave the general impression of who Christian was; controlling and relentless at times in his pursuit of me.

"I'm gonna put a stop to it," Miles said nonchalantly when I was finished.

"What does that mean?" The confusion was apparent on my face.

He shook his head and brushed it off. "Nothing bad. It's nothing to have a conversation from one man to another. No bullshit. You got nothing to worry about."

"Miles, don't do anything crazy," I pleaded.

"I won't. I'm not even mad," he assured me. He leaned in closer to me and softly kissed me on the lips. It was long and lingering. "But we don't have to worry about none of that tonight. How long has it been since we been together?"

"Too damn long," I smiled back at him as I leaned in for another kiss.

"We're gonna be a normal couple soon enough," he assured me. "I don't want you to think I was playing about leaving the game. I may not have found someone to take over for me but I've been making some moves towards it."

"Oh really?" I asked in surprise. "Like what?"

"Well, I can't just walk away. It would create a vacuum of power for people and that would mean more war. But I've been putting money to the side like crazy and I put in an application for the University of Chicago. I wanna finish my Bachelor's and maybe go back for a Masters after that."

My eyes got wide in surprise. "Wow. That's incredible. You know what you wanna major in?"

He shook his head. "Nah, not yet. I've got time to figure it out, as long as I get in of course."

"I'm sure you will." I leaned over and kiss him again. "It seems like things are finally going good for us. I'm just happy to have you back."

## CHAPTER 10

### Miles

Kallie was still asleep when I woke up the next morning. I'd given her a few orgasms the night before to make up for lost time so I knew she'd probably be knocked out for a while longer or at least until she needed to get up for work.

I slowly and carefully slid out of the bed, trying my hardest not to wake her up. I'd decided from the night before that I wanted to get up and make her some breakfast. I headed into the kitchen and started to take out everything that I'd need while trying not to make too much noise.

I didn't know if it was the sounds I was making or the smell of the food, but twenty minutes later she was up and in the kitchen with me.

"What's all this?" She asked as she came around the corner closing her robe. "You're cooking?"

"What does it look like?" I asked with a smirk. "You just worry about getting ready for work. It should be done soon enough."

"Are you sure you don't need some help?" She was skeptically looking at the pots and pans on the stove. "The bacon looks crispy enough."

"Yo chill, chill," I commanded. "I got this. Go hop in the shower." She turned around to leave the kitchen and I playfully slapped her on the butt as she left.

She came back out a few minutes later. She was dressed her clothes for work: gray slacks and a white blouse. My girl looked good in whatever she wore. She took a seat down at the table where I'd laid the food out.

"This actually looks good," she said.

"You sound surprised," I commented. "I gotta at least know my way around a kitchen a little bit. Besides, I wanted to do something special for you."

I cooked up some bacon, eggs, and cheese grits. It wasn't anything too fancy, but I knew she'd appreciate it because it came from me. I took a seat across from her and started eating my plate.

"What you got planned for the day?" she asked from across the table.

"I just got some more business to handle," I told her. "But I should be here by the time you get off later."

Her face lit up. "Really? I could get used to this."

"I hope you do," I said.

I was impressed with my cooking skills. Kallie had eaten up every single bite of her food and told me that she liked it. I enjoyed making her happy, so I was pleased. A little while later she kissed me goodbye and was on her way to work.

Once I was sure that Kallie was gone and not coming back, I grabbed my phone and made a quick call. My man Marco picked up after a few rings.

"Yo?" Marco answered.

"Yo bro, are you still on that nigga?" I asked. I was pacing the living room trying to get myself calm.

"Yeah. He's in a building. Must be for a meeting or something. But we're close to his car. He can't leave without us knowing," he explained.

I'd been livid the night before when Kallie made it clear to me that this clown nigga Christian was harassing her. I'd been so busy with everything in the streets that I didn't have any time to focus my attention on where it should have been: keeping my girl out of harm's way. I wasn't about to let that shit happen again though.

When I met that dude outside the hospital after dropping Kallie off, I knew he was trouble then and there. He didn't realize it though, but he'd told me everything I needed to know to find out more information about him.

I had one of my people do some digging into him. I soon found out that he was Christian Harper, 34 years old born and raised in Oak Park, one of the more affluent neighborhoods of Chicago. He was single, never married and had no kids. Once I got that information, I found out soon after that he also had a big of a reputation for being a ladies' man. He wasn't about to have Kallie on his list though.

The funny thing about having the information on Christian was that I didn't plan on doing anything with it, not unless I had to. People like him and people like me were really different. Just the thought of him knowing how much I knew about him would probably be enough to scare him off. It wasn't until the night before when Kallie told me everything that happened between them that I decided to make a move.

Right after Kallie went to sleep, I got up and headed into the bathroom. With the water running to cover the sound of my voice, I called up some of my people. I got them the information about dude and told them to just stay on him without letting him know he was being followed. I knew it was doing a lot but I planned to pull up on him at some point, so I wanted to keep tabs on him. I would only need to scare him into leaving Kallie and me the fuck alone.

It was clear to me that he wasn't going to stop bothering her unless someone made him stop. He was one of those types of dudes who felt like he was in control of everyone around him. I wasn't about to keep letting him think that Kallie was one of those people though.

I took a shower and got dressed. Marco sent me the address to where Christian was. When I pulled up I told my guys that I planned on following him. I wasn't expecting any trouble from him so I told them they could just hang back.

I waited outside the office building for probably another fifteen minutes or so before he made his way out. I watched from my car window as he talked on the phone and made his way around the corner to where he was parked. He got into the car and was on his way.

I assumed that he was heading back to his house. I had his address already and it was the direction that he was headed towards. I was alone in my car as I drove. I made sure to always hang back behind him by at least a car or two. It would have ruined everything if I got spotted and he called the police, especially since things between them and I had only just calmed down.

I followed close behind him, not wanting to make the journey all the way to his house. I lucked out when he made a turn down a road that had way less people on it. It was a one-way road with a wooded area next to it.

I carefully maneuvered my car so that I could get around him. My goal was to get in front of him and force him to stop. I sped up and went around his so that I was a few feet in front of him, then I short stopped. His car swerved a little to the right before he went off the road. There were no trees nearby so he didn't crash or anything. His car didn't even hit anything.

I stayed in my car and watched in the rearview mirror as he flung his car door open. He got out and I could tell he was pissed as he looked at his expensive BMW, examining it for any signs of a scratch or anything. When he didn't see any, his attention turned towards my car.

He looked like he was ready to fight, until my car door opened and I stepped out. It looked like all the hot air he was filled with had somehow left him. Slowly I made my way over to him. I was reading the expression on his face and it was one of fear, at least in his eyes.

"What the hell are you doing here?" Christian asked me. He was trying to act hard. "You're lucky nothing happened to my car."

"Nah, *you're* lucky nothing happened to your car," I asserted.

"I don't know what type of hood rat games you're trying to play but if you try anything with me, I'll have you put away for life," he declared.

I couldn't help but to laugh. I couldn't believe this clown had the nerve to try and threaten me. "Bruh, I'm not here to do nothing to you that ain't already been done to you."

"Whatever," he grumbled.

"You need to leave Kallie alone," I warned him. The smile on my face was gone and I was back to being serious.

It was his turn to laugh then. "So that's what all this is about?" He folded his arms over his chest defiantly. "I'll do whatever I wanna do when I wanna do it. But if Kallie is gonna be this much trouble then she can kiss her residency goodbye."

I took a couple of steps towards him. He must not have been a complete coward since he didn't step back. "So you're making threats now? Let me show you how you make a threat."

I reached under my t-shirt and flashed the

gun that I'd been carrying with me. The cold steel of it was starting to warm under my tight shirt.

I didn't know too much about his life growing up but for all the suits and shit he wore, Christian had heart. Boldly, he walked up a little closer to me, almost taunting me in a way.

"Leave Kallie the fuck alone," I warned him again. "Stay away from her. Like you said, y'all don't work together so you got not business with her."

Christian had a good laugh then. "Nigga, my business is whatever I want it to be. Are you mad cause I know what her pussy tastes and feels like? You know I've been to her house before too, right? I was there the other night. Did she tell you that?"

I'd had more than enough of him. I pulled my gun out of my waist and held it in my hands, pointing it towards him. I loved the fact that a lot of people talked tough but backed down as soon as a gun came out. I was only trying to scare him, but one thing I'd learned throughout the course of my life was that you only pulled a gun if you weren't afraid of using it.

Just like I knew he would, Christian took a couple of steps back and held up his hands.

"What happened bro? You was just talkin' crazy," I said.

Much to my surprise, Christian had more fight in him than I'd imagine. Quicker than I thought he could move, he stretched his hand out and tried to grab for the gun. The suddenness of the move caught me off guard and before I knew it, the gun had gone off.

Christian took a step back and then stumbled back even further. He backed up till he was almost at his car and then fell back towards it. He was wearing a navy-blue suit with a light blue shirt underneath. I could already see that it was starting to dark with his blood.

I thought about just leaving the scene but I couldn't do that. I ran back to my car and grabbed one of the spare burner phones that I kept in the glove compartment. I took out one of the ones that I never used before and put on a pair of gloves that I had.

I walked back over to Christian whose eyes were focused on me. I could tell that he was starting to have trouble breathing as he grabbed at his chest. I dialed 911 on the phone with a gloved hand and then threw the phone down next to him.

I kneeled down in front of him and shook my head. "You should live if the ambulance comes in enough time," I remarked.

I was surprised that none of my security people had come running. I was sure that they'd heard the gunshot. It was better for them not to come though since I had some cleaning up to do. I made sure that my fingerprints weren't on the phone since I used gloves and I made sure to retrace my steps in the dirt and clear them away. I didn't need any traces that I'd been there.

I was in my car and gone before I even heard the sirens of the ambulance.

## Kallie

I LOOKED DOWN at my pager which was going off for the second time in the span of a few minutes. I was upstairs working on a patient, but I was getting called to go down to the Emergency Room. I wasn't scheduled to be there today, which meant I was either needed on a consult or they were backed up and could use more people.

When I finally made my way down there it turned out it was the latter. I checked in with a nurse and she explained that there had been a bad car accident. People were being taken to whatever hospitals could take them. I looked around our E.R. and noticed all the people on beds all over.

Being in the emergency room required good judgement. People came in there every day with things ranging from phantom pains and sore throats to masses on their body and limbs in need of repair. I went ahead and got started sorting through the patients of the car crash, trying to see who needed the most urgent care. I knew that I'd probably spend the rest of my shift there.

I was working on one of the drivers of a car. He wasn't as badly injured as one of the others. He did have a couple of scratches and his broken his ankle, but other than that he was cool. I let him know that we'd be with him after a while. The more pressing issues came from the people who had head injuries. Those could go from bad to worse if we didn't run the right tests.

I was working on trying to get some information from one of the passengers of one of the cars when I heard a scream. Someone yelling that way in an emergency room wasn't something that we normally heard. The scream was blood curdling and sent a chill threw me because I immediately recognized the person whose voice it was.

I let the patient I was with know that I'd be right back as I went to investigate. Stella never screamed that way, so I needed to figure out why it happened. I made my way over to where she was, close to the entrance. She was looking down at someone on a stretcher as she pushed it towards the back.

I looked down and realized why she'd screamed. Christian was laying on the stretcher. His shirt was open revealing a gunshot wound. His breathing was shallow and his eyes were closed.

"Oh my God. Christian!" I called out to him trying to wake him. The EMT's who'd brought him in looked at Stella and I like we were crazy but went on rambling off his stats.

"Male, mid 30's. Gunshot wound to the

abdomen. We've been unsuccessful in stopping the bleeding and there is no exit wound present," one of them said.

I was emotional, but I knew what needed to be done. As we wheeled him to the the back I took a deep breath and went into action mode. He was close to losing his life. I didn't have time to ask questions about how he'd gotten shot or anything. The important thing was making sure that Christian didn't die.

"He's lost a lot of blood!" I declared to the team of people working around me. I grabbed the sheet under his body and helped another doctor lift him and move him to a more secure bed. "I need two pints of O negative. The bullet hasn't exited yet. We need to prep an O.R."

"Stay with me," I pleaded as I leaned down and spoke into Christian's ear.

# CHAPTER 11

As a doctor working in a hospital, there are certain sounds that you get used to hearing. Names of diseases and medications, groans and moans, and tears of either laughter or heartbreak are all things that you become accustomed to hearing. You also get used to the slow or sometimes quick beeps that a machine makes.

When you see the slow beeping of a heart rate and pulse monitor on a TV screen, you always imagine what it would be like in a moment like that if you were somehow involved. What would be the case if you or someone you knew were hooked up to one of those machines? As I sat next to Christian's bed, listening to the rhythmic machine keep its pace, thoughts went through my mind. I'd come very close to hearing the machines he was hooked up to flatline and it had been terrifying for me.

Christian came into the Emergency Room of my hospital with a gunshot wound. He was covered in blood, struggling to breathe, and on the verge of death. The bullet entered through his abdomen but pierced his arm. He was covered in so much blood that it was hard to tell where the wound had come from.

Christian had made it to the hospital in enough time to be saved, thank God. I didn't know any of the details of what happened to him but the wounds he'd sustained weren't bad enough to kill him. The issue was that he'd lost so much blood that he'd almost died on the operating table. He'd lost so much that his body ended up going into shock and we'd nearly lost him.

I shuddered just thinking about it again. It was cold in the room, but my chill came from my thoughts. Tears welled up in my eyes as I replayed the scene over and over again in my head.

*"He's lost a lot of blood!" I declared to the team of*

*people working around me. I grabbed the sheet under his body and helped another doctor lift him and move him to a more secure bed. "I need two pints of O negative. The bullet hasn't exited yet. We need to prep an O.R."*

*"Stay with me," I pleaded as I leaned down and spoke into Christian's ear.*

*I knew that I couldn't let my emotions get in the way. Stella seemed to have snapped out of her shock for the moment because she was heading in my direction. Myself and the nurses around me worked as a team. We cut open his shirt to remove it from his body so that we could see where he'd been shot and how bad it was.*

*I turned him just to confirm what the EMT's said. I didn't see an exit wound. I knew then that it must have been bad.*

*"Your foot!" someone called out. I didn't know who they were talking to until I looked up and realized it was me. A nurse was pointing down towards my feet. I looked down to see that there was blood dripping down onto me from Christian's outstretched arm.*

*"That's what happened," I announced as I held up his arm. "The bullet entered and exited the abdomen but it pierced his arm." It made sense to me then. The wound in his abdomen was bad but not bad but his arm was worse. He was starting to look more pale.*

*We had to take him up to the operating room in order*

*to stop the bleeding. We also needed to check for and remove any fragments of the bullet as well as fix his arm. It would probably be months, if ever, before it worked again the right way.*

*We worked for a few hours. There were a few tiny pieces of bullet in his arm that were causing more bleeding. If we didn't get them all, the results could have been dangerous.*

It was touch and go for a while. The amount of blood that he'd lost was insane. I didn't know if he'd been drinking or something but it almost seemed thinner than usual. We gave him an entire pint and it still wasn't enough. When it was all said and done, we decided to keep him sedated.

While he was on the operating table, I looked down at his face that was full of life and saw how pale it was. His body temperature had dropped and he'd been cold to the touch. As far as I knew, it was the closest to death he'd ever come. The image of it would forever be burned in my mind.

When he came out of surgery, we moved him up to a private room in the Intensive Care Unit. His family had been notified and they'd been with him all night long, only having just left not too long ago with a promise to return. I took that as my chance to pop into the room and check on him.

Christian was on a lot of medications and it would probably be a few days before anyone felt safe enough to start to take him off of them. He was also still getting blood transfusions because of what he'd lost. There was even talk of another surgery because he might have some scarring inside that was bleeding. It was still kind of touch and go.

My phone vibrated again in the top pocket of my lab coat. It had been doing it off and on all day long, but I couldn't answer. Between the victims of the car crash that had flooded our emergency room and then dealing with Christian, I didn't have any time to try and be social with anyone. I was way too focused on doing my job and making sure that Christian didn't die on the table.

Now that I finally had a couple of moments to breathe, I pulled my phone out to check it. It turned out to be Miles, just as I'd figured. I looked at Christian's sleeping body and then answered the phone.

"Yo I—" Miles began, but I cut him off.

"Miles," I cried into the phone, letting out so many of the emotions that I'd been keeping inside the last few hours, "something bad happened to Christian."

"Calm down. Your voice is breaking up," he said in a soft tone.

I was crying but it was on the verge of become a full-on sobbing fit. "Christian got shot!" I announced. I started pacing back and forth in the room. I was on the phone talking to Miles but it felt like I was just saying my own thoughts out loud. "I don't know how this could've happened. Why would he even be around a gun? I heard some stuff from the cops that came to visit and it wasn't even a robbery.

"I mean yeah, he got on my nerves some-times but I would *never* wish death on anyone. I just can't believe something like this happened to him. It was so hard to operate on him. My hands were shaking. I almost got emotional in the operating room but I had to keep it togeth-er," I finished. I took a deep breath to try and calm myself down. I felt like I was going to have a panic attack or something like that.

"Don't get yourself too worked up," Miles said in an effort to calm me down. He took a deep breath and let it out into the phone. "I gotta tell you something."

"What is it?" I asked. I couldn't deal with any more bad news but if he was bringing it up at a time like this then I knew it must have been really bad.

"I just... I just need you to hear me out," Miles stammered through his sentence. I didn't know why he sounded so nervous all of a sudden, but it was starting to freak me out.

"Miles, what happened?" I demanded to know. "Just spit it out already."

"I went to see Christian," he announced. He got silent after that. His words hung heavy in the air.

It felt like all the air in my body left. I had to quickly plop down in the chair I was sitting in before or else I would have fallen over. "You went to see Christian?" I asked in confusion. "What do... why would you go to see Christian?"

"I told you I wanted to talk to him about all the stuff with y'all. All I wanted to do was talk to him," Miles was saying quickly. I think he wanted to get it all out before I had a chance to interrupt him. "He was talkin' all types of bullshit when I got there. He was making threats, talkin' about how you were gonna lose your residency cause of the drama and shit. He started saying he was gonna make sure I went to jail for life. I ain't have no intention on shooting that man. I swear I only pulled out the gun to scare him. He grabbed for it and then it went off."

I couldn't say anything. You know the feeling of being so angry that you know the only thing you can do is scream? That was me at that moment. I got up and ran out of the room to find somewhere else to go. I went down a hall or two and found an unlocked janitors' closet in a mostly empty hallway. Luckily for me the closet was a deep one so the chances of people hearing me when I went off were low.

My heart was racing in my chest. I felt my hands get all sweaty and clammy. I felt a little light headed. It was all just too much for me.

"Miles, are you fucking serious?" I screamed into the phone. "I can't believe you. Do you know what you've done? Do you know what could happen? Did you even think about ANY OF IT?" I knew someone probably heard me but at that point I didn't give a single fuck.

"Kallie I'm—" He tried to say something but I wasn't done yet.

"Don't say you're sorry!" I fumed into the phone. "You can't just be sorry for doing something like this. A man almost died! Someone I know almost died cause you didn't know how to listen to me. Christian is almost dead. I can't believe this shit. I don't know if I can forgive you, Miles. I really don't."

"So what are you say—"

"I'll talk to you later." I pulled the phone from my ear and pressed the end button.

I couldn't contain myself. I felt like I was on the verge of exploding or something. My head felt light all of a sudden. It almost felt like I was going to pass out. I had to take a couple of deep breaths just calm myself enough to leave the closet. Once I came out I headed down the hall to the nearest single bathroom. I didn't want to deal with anyone else.

I walked in and locked the door behind me. I'd arrived right on time, too. The waves that had been spinning in my stomach sent my headed straight to the toilet. I raised the lid in just enough time to manage not to get any vomit on it.

I kneeled there on my knees trying to see if it would happen again, and all I could do was think. Miles shot Christian. Miles shot Christian. The thoughts replayed over and over in my head.

*You know it's your fault,* I thought to myself. I couldn't help but to think it. Yeah, Miles might have been the one behind the trigger but I might as well have done it myself. There were so many layers to it and I just kept wondering what if. What if I'd never messed around with Miles? What if Christian woke up and wanted to talk to the police? Thoughts swirled around in my head.

After I was sure that I was done throwing up, I stood up and headed to the sink. I gargled my mouth out with some water and made a note to head to my bag to get my toothbrush so I could brush my teeth. I ran cold water in the sink and splashed some on my face. I was just trying to calm myself down.

Somehow, I managed to finish my shift. It had taken a lot of convincing to do it but I managed to talk myself into staying. Usually I could just throw myself into my work to get my mind off of things but all anyone wanted to talk about was Christian. My only comfort came from being in the room with my patients.

When my shift ended I headed straight up to Christian's room to sit with him. He was still unconscious and unaware of my presence, but it was important *to me* for me to be there. I was racked with guilt. I kept replaying the conversation with Miles over and over again.

I vowed to myself that I would do anything and everything that I could in order to help Christian get better. I'd thanked God more than a few times that day for the fact that Christian survived.

As I sat by Christian's bedside, my cell phone lit up again. It had gotten so bad that I had to turn the vibration off. It was Miles calling, probably trying to explain himself or apologize. In all honesty, I wasn't in the mood to talk to him. I'd been thinking about it all day long and I realized that for as much as I cared about Miles and how well he treated me, he was also still somewhat of a burden. My relationship with Stella was almost nonexistent. Christian had been shot. Miles was the cause of those problems. I could almost excuse his drug dealing but this was a whole different level of things.

**CHAPTER 12**

I ended up staying with Christian till pretty late into the night. It was well after midnight when I finally headed home. I hadn't planned on staying so late, but I ended up falling asleep after sitting by his bedside for so long. It worked out for me anyway though because I was off the following day.

I drove back to my apartment in silence. I didn't want the radio or anything. I just needed to be alone with my thoughts, and there were a lot of them. I pulled up at a stop light and slammed my hands on the steering wheel a few times in frustration. I didn't even know what I was mad about specifically, everything just seemed to be a mess. I felt like I was losing control.

I hated that Christian had gotten shot. It didn't matter if it was Miles or anyone else. Whatever he and I'd been through before didn't really matter to me. I could only deal with the present and the facts as they were presented to me.

Miles must have finally taken my hint. He hadn't called me anymore in the last few hours. I still kept my vibrations off though because I knew that there was every chance that he'd start right back up if I gave him a chance to. I somehow managed to get a decent night's sleep, despite everything that had taken place that day.

The following morning, I was coming back into my building from a run. I'd managed to way up extra early without trying and even though I tried to go back to sleep for over an hour, nothing worked. Finally, I just decided to get up and workout. Running alone by myself in the early morning sun was a quick, albeit temporary, fix to my problems. I managed to forget about everything as I ran but as I made my way back home, I realized that there were still some problems you couldn't outrun.

I was still half a block away from my apartment building when I spotted a tall figure standing outside of it. He was leaning against the outside of the building looking as nonchalant as he could manage. I immediately recognized Miles. I was surprised to see him standing there. Pop-ups were never usually his thing, but I guessed that he was making an exception since the situation called for it.

He awkwardly turned to me as he spotted me coming down the block. I was about to keep on walking right passed him but he called out to me. He said my name forcefully. I didn't doubt that he probably would have followed me into the building if I'd have let him. I didn't want him to make a scene, nor did I need any nosey neighbors in the lobby being all up in my business. I stopped and turned around. Finally, I motioned for him to follow behind me.

I let Miles in because I wanted to know *all* the details of what happened between him and Christian. I felt like I would go crazy if I didn't. I think in my mind if I heard the entire story, I might be able to find some silver lining in it. I knew it was dumb but I had to keep my hopes up. The truth was owed to me. I deserved at least that much. In the back of my mind though, I knew that there probably wouldn't be any explanation that could justify the shooting, at least not any reason that I'd be able to condone.

Miles and I didn't say a word to one another as we headed up to my apartment. We were on opposite sides of the elevator, each of us leaned against the cold metallic walls. I was staring at him so hard that I was sure I was going to bore a hole into him. He was making a conscious effort not to look at me even though I was sure he could feel my gaze on him. We got into my apartment and before he had a chance to sit down and get comfortable, I turned on him.

"So, what do you want, Miles?" I asked. I folded my arms across my chest. The expression on my face must have let him know that he didn't have any time to bullshit. He needed to get right to the point.

He took a deep breath. "Yo, just wanted to talk to you face to face. I needed to tell you I'm sorry in person. I know I owe you an explanation and an apology."

"I'm not the one you should be apologizing

to," I snapped at him. It felt like the room was getting hotter. My blood was staring to boil.

"I know, I know," he said "How is Christian doing? I want you to know that I ain't never wanna kill him. I was even the one who called the ambulance. I knew how much it would hurt you if he died."

I rolled my eyes. I couldn't believe he was standing there trying to make it seem like he'd done something good by calling the ambulance. He wouldn't have had to if he hadn't been there. I still couldn't believe everything that was happening.

"It hurts as much knowing he got shot by you," I snapped. "I'm so disappointed in you."

I could tell that my words stung Miles. I almost felt bad but then I remembered why we were talking and it made me feel justified. The more I stood there thinking about it, the more upset I got. I couldn't believe that Miles called the ambulance and then had the nerve to make it seem like he was doing Christian a favor. It was the absolute least he could do since he'd almost ended his life.

"Actually Miles, we can't do this right now," I dismissed him. I unfolded my arms and headed towards the door to open it. "You should go."

"But I just got here," he said in frustration. "Are you serious right now? You can't be. You just said you wanted to hear what I had to say. "

"And I do... but not today," I announced. "I need time to myself to think about some stuff."

Miles sighed and headed towards the door. "You gotta be joking." He shook his head at me. "Are you gonna at least answer me if I call you?"

I shrugged nonchalantly. "Honestly, I don't know," I responded. He stepped outside into the hallway. I could see that he had something else to say. Before he could open his mouth again, I closed the door on him and turned to head to the shower.

I was off from work that day, but I was still heading to the hospital anyways. I wanted to spend time with Christian. A part of me felt like I *needed* to spend time with Christian. I was feeling guilty. I might as well have pulled the trigger myself so the least I could do was be there for him. The same way that I'd helped Miles out, I wanted to do the same for him. I knew that it was nothing more than my guilt about the situation but either way, I needed to be there.

I worked myself into a routine that revolved around the hospital, just in a different capacity than it was in before. When I had a shift, I worked it as usual. Afterwards I could usually be found in Christian's room. He would survive but he wasn't out of the woods yet. It was still very touch and go and his recovery time looked like it could go on for a while.

One day my doorman commented on how he hadn't been seeing much of me anymore. In all honesty, I'd only been coming home to get clothes and head back to work. The staff had a full locker room so showering there was something that everyone did. It usually only happened between shifts, but I did it between my shifts and my visits with Christian.

Miles had been calling me every day. It wasn't nonstop like it had been before, but it was clear to me that he wasn't going to stop. I hadn't answered once since that day we'd last spoken. It had been an entire week since we'd spoken, the longest in all the time that we'd known one another. I even tried to minimize how often I went home in case he decided to pull another pop up. Each time I went I tried to grab enough clothes to last me for a day or two so that I wouldn't have to come back.

I had to head back to my apartment one day to grab some more clothes and drop off the dirty ones. It had become normal for me to just pop in. I walked into my place and was about to head to the bedroom when I noticed the TV was on. Miles was sitting on the couch and turned to face me. He looked pretty damned comfortable for someone who hadn't been invited.

"What are you doing here?" I asked in shock. "How'd you get in?" I was ready to go off on my doorman. I couldn't believe that he'd let someone into my apartment without talking to me about it first. He was only supposed to do that if I gave him instructions to do so.

Miles stood up and reached into his pocket to pull something out. "You must've forgotten you gave me a key."

I nodded in understanding. "Oh shit. I really did." About a month or two earlier I gave Miles a key to my place. It hadn't been a big deal or anything like that. I just knew that if he was coming in at odd times of night, he needed a key so he wouldn't have to wake me up. My doorman didn't work all night long either and I didn't need anyone calling the police on a strange looking Black man hanging out outside of the building trying to get in. It had been a matter of convenience. I didn't even remember that he had it because he'd never used it before.

"I see," he said with a shake of his head.

"Well, at least you're only just now using it," I commented. I turned and made a beeline straight for my bedroom. I was trying to get as far away from him as possible. I knew that the only reason Miles had come was because I hadn't been speaking to him.

Miles sped up and walked ahead of me to block my way. I tried to step around him but he blocked me with his arm.

"Can you move?" I asked. I took a step back and sized him up as if I was any kind of a threat to him.

"Can you just listen?" he shot back. The look on his face let me know that he was determined to stand there all night if he needed to. I could wait it out but I was tired from my day.

I sighed and then took a step back. "Go on Miles. What do you have to say?"

Miles looked relieved. I was glad that he didn't mess around and got straight to it. "Baby, I know you don't wanna hear how sorry I am, but I am sorry. I messed up real bad. I only wanted to scare that nigga. I had some of my people follow behind him, just keeping tabs on him, nothing major. So I followed behind him and when I got a chance, I got out the car to speak to him."

Miles paused and waited to see if I was listening. I headed back into the living room and sat down on a couch. He tried to sit next to me but I stopped him and sent him to another chair. He went over to it and took a seat facing me. As he spoke he made sure to look me in the eyes.

"I wasn't mad at the nigga. I knew he was a tough talker but it's not like he could have hurt me," Miles went on. "I ain't even care about him making threats about me like that. But when he started talking about how he remembered fucking you and all this other shit about how he was gonna make sure you lost your job...I just wanted to scare him."

"So then how'd he end up getting shot?" I asked. I was still missing some piece of the puzzle. It didn't sound like Miles was lying, but there was clearly more to it than he was letting on.

"I swear to God, I don't know," he said in a way that sounded serious. He hadn't taken his eyes off of me. If he was lying, he was doing a great job. "I pulled the gun out to scare him. I pointed it at him but he wasn't scared, or if he was, I couldn't tell. He walked right up to that shit like it was nothing. He reached out; I don't know to hit me or what but when he moved, I moved, and the gun went off. The safety wasn't on like I thought."

"That's a lot," was all I could muster up to say. I didn't know how I felt about his explanation even though his words seemed sincere. "That's a whole lot."

"You know how much I've been working on changing," Miles stated. "Why would I wanna jeopardize that by doing some dumb shit? I just got the cops off of me from all that mess from before. You know I'm trying to leave all this shit behind so I could be the man you actually need; someone legit, not a nigga in the streets. I just got so pissed off when it seemed like he was about to take away everything that you worked for."

Miles was right; he had been working hard to try and improve himself. He made it clear that he wanted out of the game. I knew that I wasn't the only cause of it. He wanted to get out of it for himself and that was important. He raised some valid points in his argument which led me to the conclusion that it did.

I believed Miles. I don't know what it was, but I did. It could have been the way he told the story or the fact that nothing in his face said that he was lying. I just didn't want to believe that Christian had turned into such a person in the moment like that. I knew he could be pompous and arrogant but making a full-blown threat about my job was something else. I also didn't know how he all of a sudden became so bold as to walk up to the barrel of a gun.

"Oh God," I sighed heavily. I leaned back on the couch and closed my eyes. I put my hand on my head and started to massage my temple. More thoughts. All I seemed to do that week was overthink. When I opened my eyes they'd gotten a bit watery from the emotions I'd been feeling.

Miles got up and walked over to me, sitting himself down on the couch next to me. He reached out slowly to touch me and when he saw that I didn't fight him, he wrapped his arm around me. His scent filled my nose as I let myself lean a little onto his shoulders. It was one of those times when I was glad to have someone else around.

"Yo, I'm so sorry you're going through all this," he said in comfort. "I never wanted any of this for you. I'm gonna fix this."

I was on the verge of having a full-blown breakdown. "Miles, you should go. I just wanna be alone," I said, weakly. I felt out of it. I just wanted to lay down for a while and not get up.

"I know you better than that," he responded. He pulled me a little bit closer to him, holding me tight. It may not have been what I wanted but it was what I needed. "I got you."

## CHAPTER 13

Miles and I sat on the couch for the next few minutes in silence. His strong arms were wrapped around my waist in a way that comforted me. His hand was gripping mine tightly as if he would never let go. It was all nothing short of what I needed in the moment. I felt like I was on the verge of breaking down and I didn't know how to stop myself. It felt like Miles and I had gone from the frying pan into the fire.

After a few more minutes Miles finally got up. Much to my surprise, he kneeled down and picked me up off of the couch like I was nothing. Holding me in his arms, he slowly walked me to the bedroom and laid me down. I didn't put up any fight. He headed into the bathroom and I could hear the sounds of the tub filling up with water.

I got up and started to get undressed. He came back into the bedroom a few minutes later to grab me. When I walked into the bathroom I was surprised to see that he'd also lit some candles. The floral smells of them filled the air as I stepped into the warm bath.

"I know you're tired," Miles comforted me as he helped me into the tub. It was nothing short of romantic the way he sat in there with me. He helped me wash my back and every-thing. It was romantic but also incredibly inti-mate, probably more intimate than anything we'd done before.

When I got out of the tub, Miles led me back into the bedroom. He helped me mois-turize my skin with some coconut oil and even gave me a little massage. He laid in the bed next to me when we were done.

I figured he was trying to give me some space since he wasn't trying to cuddle with me. The issue was that I didn't want to still feel alone with him being so close. I reached out and grabbed his shirt to try and pull him closer to me. He resisted a little but finally snuggled up to me.

I ran my leg up his body and rested it across his waist. Leaning into him a little bit more, I started to plant soft kisses all on his lips and face.

"You should take a nap," he insisted. "You've been through a lot."

I ignored him and leaned in again, this time only going for his lips. At first he didn't kiss back, but after a couple more seconds, he must've figured out that I wasn't going to stop. I rested my hand on Miles' face as we kissed. I'd even started to move my body closer to his. His hand was creeping up my thigh when I suddenly pulled my head back from his.

"What happened?" he asked. He must have been surprised by my suddenness.

"I just... it's nothing." I tried to dismiss it. I leaned my head closer to his to keep on kissing him but he just backed up some. He raised his eyebrow at me and I sighed. "I just have a bad feeling about this."

Miles immediately took his hand off of me. "I told you we ain't have to do anything. I know you're tired."

I shook my head at him. "Not *this*," I indicated. "I mean all this stuff with Christian."

"What's on your mind?" he asked.

"I'm still trying to wrap my head around all of it. I just can't believe that this man I *thought* I knew pretty well could be this type of guy," I began to explain. "If he was out here making threats about my residency, then I know for sure he wouldn't hesitate to have you locked up if he got the chance."

"I know what you mean," he said with a sigh. "I've been thinking about it. Don't think I haven't. Thankfully he didn't die, but it's still attempted murder. All that only comes into play if I get caught though, and I don't plan on letting that happen."

"How would you do that? We don't know what's gonna happen," I responded.

"Trust me," he replied. "I could come up with an alibi if need be. It wouldn't be the first time I was in a tough position. If it comes down to it, I promise I'll do whatever I gotta do to get back to you."

Listening to Miles' words made me think about something else that had been bugging me for a while. The police hadn't gotten involved.

At all. No one had come asking any questions at the hospital as far as I knew. No one had come forward putting Miles close to the scene or anything, so they hadn't been looking for him either. I just wondered when the other shoe was going to drop. I was starting to get a clearer picture of who Christian was and I knew that he wouldn't hesitate if need be to put Miles away.

"There you go again," Miles' voice snapped me from my thoughts.

"What you mean?" I asked.

"You keep getting lost in your thoughts. You need to rest." Miles reached down and grabbed my hand. "Stop worrying. I can handle whatever happens next. At the end of the day, I'm man enough to know that these are my consequences. I gotta be able to face 'em, but that doesn't mean that you need to be worrying about me."

Miles words seemed to give me some level of comfort. I knew I wouldn't *stop* worrying but I could probably worry a lot less than I was. No matter what happened, all either one of us could do was wait and see what happened. Christian might wake up and have forgotten all the details, or he could get up and head straight for the police. Only time would tell.

Miles was right about one thing. I was tired for sure. It felt like I was running on fumes. However, there was one way that I knew for sure that I could sleep like a baby.

I ran my fingers along Miles' bare chest, slowly circling each of his nipples before I leaned in and began to kiss him passionately. I knew he would try and stop me, so I applied more force to the kiss to stop him from doing it. I knew that I should have probably just went to sleep but I wanted to feel good and I knew that Miles could help me out with that.

His hand creeped up my bare thigh until it reached my ass. He grabbed handful of it and squeezed its plumpness before tapping it a few times with his hand to make it jiggle. Miles loved my ass and always found ways to remind me of it.

Miles was slow and gentle as he moved his body. Instead of asking me to turn around, he moved himself so that he could lay behind me. His tall frame almost went off the bed. I could feel his breathing on my neck as he cocked my head to the side to he could start to lick and suck at my neck. It felt like the room was getting warmer.

I could feel the semi-hardness of Miles' dick starting to press me in the back. He reached around me, first playing with my breasts for a few minutes before he let his hands disappear into my panties. Miles stuck a finger inside me, slowly and skillfully. He didn't even move it at first. He let me grind my legs on it. After a few minutes of that, he took charge, inserting another one.

The combination of Miles fingering me and licking on my neck in a way that I was sure would leave me with a hickey was turning me on like crazy. I couldn't help but to grind my hips back on him.

I almost hungry as I reached behind me to tug at the pants he was wearing. I managed to unbuckle his pants and pull them down a little bit before he finished the job for me.

"Put in in, Miles," I moaned to him. He wrapped his hand around my neck and turned my head around so I could kiss him better. His jeans were still wrapped around his ankles as he slowly pushed his hardness into me. No matter how often we had sex, I was always taken by aback by the size of his dick.

"Fuck," I moaned again as I felt the familiar mix of pressure and pleasure that could only come from him being all the way inside of me. Miles slowly started to grind his hips, moving himself in and out of me. He started off slowly but after a while he'd built up a rhythm and was moving faster.

The sounds of our skin slapping together mixed with Miles' hands around my neck sent my body to shaking. He'd only been stroking me for a couple of minutes when I felt the familiar and pleasant sensation of my orgasm. My body got hot and it felt like I was tingling all over.

"Ahh!" I cried out in pleasure. Miles only stopped moving for a few moments to let me catch my breath before he started back up. This time he was a bit more aggressive. It felt like he was trying to let out all the stress and frustration that he'd been holding onto for the last few days.

"Damn baby," he growled in my ear. "Ahh shit!" He cried out as he exploded. I felt the familiarity of his body speeding up and slowing down before he finally stopped. His deep breathing was warm in my ear. Miles and I got cleaned up and I drifted off to sleep.

## Miles

You know how you jump out of bed if you hear something too loud and it startles you? That was how I woke up in the middle of the night. I jumped up and sat up like someone had scared the shit out of me or something. It was dark but my eyes shot open. It only took me a few seconds to remember when, and where, I'd fallen asleep. Kallie and I had just finished making love and the two of us drifted off with one another in her bed.

It was the middle of the night but the light of the city was still bright. Some of them shined through the window, casting their glow over the two of us. Kallie had moved over some in her sleep, so she was closer to the window. I turned over onto my side and watched her sleep. She was beautiful, even when she was sleeping, no one could ever deny that.

*I'm so used to this,* I thought to myself as I laid

there next to her. I'd become so accustomed to moments like these. I never really let myself get too close to women. I'd fuck 'em and move on, for the most part. Kallie was something else though. She carried herself in a way that made her stand out. She treated me good and only ever wanted what was best for me. I'd become so used to being around her and spending time with her that the fear that it all might get taken away was constantly on my mind.

I started to let my mind wander. I laid there and imagined what it would be like without her. I didn't know what was gonna happen when Christian was feeling better but I knew I'd have to face it at some point.

My mind was going over all the possibilities that it could handle. I could end up having to go to jail. I could end up on the run or something like that.

*Nah, not gonna happen,* I thought to myself. Regardless of whatever, I wasn't going to jail. I promised myself in that moment that I needed to do whatever I needed to do to avoid jail.

I wasn't about to kill Christian or anything like that. I knew that Kallie would be devastated if that ever happened, not to mention what the ramifications of it would be. I needed to start off by getting rid of the gun I'd used to shoot Christian. It was stupid on my fault to still have it but I was so caught up in shit that I hadn't had a chance to ditch it. I made a mental note just then that I would need to wipe it down and then get rid of it.

The only other thing I would need was an alibi—an airtight one. I knew that I wouldn't be able to come up with something right then and there, but I planned on having one, just in case.

I moved a little closer to Kallie and wrapped my arm around her, pulling her closer to me. Her hair smelled like fruits as she backed her body into mine. The comfort that I felt from being around her made me feel like I was on top of the world. I didn't need the game and everything that came with it as long as I had her by my side. I'd fucked up in a major way. I knew that we hadn't even gotten close to really seeing what the future held for us, but I planned on doing everything that I could in order to make sure that we'd be together.

I pushed all the thoughts out of my head as I let myself drift off to sleep, hoping that the next day would be better than the one before it.

CHAPTER 14

## Kallie

I got up a little early and decided to leave Miles sleeping while I headed off to work. He had a key so I knew that he would let himself out whenever he wanted to. The night before had been a lot for the both of us. I knew that I was still feeling the after effects. Emotions were running high. I still had a lot on my mind but I was at least able to say that I was starting to make some progress in processing them.

The conversation with Miles played over and over again in my head. I couldn't believe the lengths that Christian would go to. I felt bad for even thinking it but a part of me slightly felt like he might have deserved to be shot. Every time the thought popped into my head I quickly dismissed it. I felt bad about it but every time I thought about his threats to me, I felt myself getting angry.

I got to work on time and changed into my lab coat. I headed upstairs to check in on Christian. I was going to be his attending for the day so I needed to be there.

I got to Christian's room and was surprised to see Stella sitting in the chair by his bed when I arrived. She'd been looking down at her phone but looked up when she saw me. She'd been with him overnight. She must have been hanging out in his room until the next shift arrived to relieve her.

"Good morning," I said in a monotone. Stella and I had taken to avoiding one another for the most part but if we were face to face there was no reason we couldn't speak.

"Morning," she replied as she stood up. Walking passed the foot of his bed, she grabbed his chart and headed towards me. "He's doing alright. There haven't really been any changes. We're keeping him in the medically induced sleep while we run some more tests to figure out what's going on with his blood. Once we wake him up though, we'll be severely reducing the meds. He's gonna be in some pain but it should be manageable."

"Thank you," I said to her. "Did you fall asleep here?"

Stella nodded her head. "You know the VIPs get the best rooms in the hospital. They're the best place to take a nap." She managed to smile at me a little, which made me feel good.

I opened up my mouth to say something but was interrupted by a group of people coming into the room. There were four of them; three men and a woman. I scanned the group and quickly realized that two of the men were police officers. They were dressed in oversized suits and I noticed their badges gleaming.

"Mrs. Harper, are you sure your son didn't have any enemies?" one of the detectives asked. The officer was a handsome older man who looked Latino. He had tan skin and salt and pepper hair that was cut low. He was sporting a goatee and it looked like he kept himself in shape, from the look of his arms.

The woman had come into the room and immediately headed towards Christian's bedside.

She looked down at him, her eyes filled with tears that didn't fall. She placed her hand on Christian's head and stroked his hair a few times before finally turning around to address him and his question.

"He didn't have any enemies," she scoffed at him. She didn't look like Christian, at least not at first. Her cocoa colored skin and dark brown hair weren't like his but the longer I looked at her, the more of him I saw.

"We've already gone over this," said the man who'd been silent the entire time. It was *very* obvious that he was Christian's father. He looked like an older version of him, just a little taller with a little more weight. He was nowhere close to being fat or anything. "Look, I know you probably get a lot of calls about a lot of Black men shot in Chicago. My son is a well-respected businessman, not some corner store thug like you've been implying."

"We're just trying to get to the bottom of this," the Latino detective said. Between him and his partner I couldn't really tell who was in charge. I got the sense that they played off of one another to throw people off balance.

"We don't mean anything by our line of

questioning," his partner chimed in. "We just have to look at it from all angles. He was shot at a close range and nothing was taken. That implies that he probably knew, or at least knew of whoever shot him."

Having the police right in front of me had sent me into an inward panic. I knew that they wanted to get to the bottom of things. It wasn't as though Christian was a nobody. His family had a lot of money which also meant a lot of power in the city of Chicago.

I'd been wondering for a while why the police hadn't come around sooner, but in that moment, I finally got my answer. It seemed like Christian's parents had been keeping them away. It made sense since he wouldn't be able to answer any questions.

I listened intently to everything the officers were saying. I was taking mental notes of the things they did and didn't say so that I could piece together my own thoughts. From what I could gather, they had no suspects or anything like that. It seemed like the biggest piece of evidence would have to come from Christian himself and since he was asleep, they had nothing. I supposed that should have made me happy or something, but it didn't.

"We'll be by to talk again once he wakes up," said the Latino detective. He took a look at Christian before nodding politely at his parents and heading out of the room followed by his partner.

Stella and I had been standing in the room in a sort of awkward silence. No one had acknowledged us in the slightest. I finally cleared my throat, causing his parents to finally look up at Stella and me.

I headed towards Christian's parents, extending my hand to them. "Hello Mr. and Mrs. Harper. My name is Kallie Jameson. I'm one of the doctors taking care of your son. I want to assure you that Christian is getting the best care possible."

His mother looked down at my hand before grabbing it, shaking it, and letting it go quickly. "Oh, *you're Kallie*," she said snootily. "It's nice to put a name to a face. I guess he probably is getting the best care if you're the one taking care of him."

Christian's father grabbed my hand and shook it. He was apparently the nicer of the two of them. "Please forgive my wife. She's been a bit emotional, for obvious reasons. I'm Gerald and this is my wife, Michelle."

"It's a pleasure to meet you both," I said. I wanted to ask his wife what she apparently knew about me, but I was in doctor mode and needed to be professional. "I want you to know that we're doing everything that we can for Christian. He has the best care in the hospital."

"We can't thank you enough for saving our son's life," Gerald said. There was a genuine look on his face that made me feel warm, but also guilty about knowing the truth about *how* their son's life had come to need saving.

"It's my job," I said, modestly. It was a strange position to be in; Christian had apparently spoken to his parents about me, but I didn't know anything about them.

"Well, we did always hear you were good at your job," Michelle chimed in. "And I mean, who's going to work harder to save someone's life than someone they used to sleep with?"

If I was drinking something I would have choked or spit it out. I don't know if this was something that she normally did but I was feeling awkward as hell. I felt my face get warm.

I was glad that everyone in the room, including Stella, was already aware of Christian and I. Otherwise I would have been more self-conscious. Either way, the old woman had some nerve.

"Michelle," Gerald's voice growled out a warning to her before he redirected his attention back to me. "Excuse her. What she meant to say was that Christian mentioned you before. He always said you were good at your job."

I was definitely surprised to know that they knew so much about me, especially considering that Christian had never mentioned them to me at all. "That's good to hear."

I was glad in that moment for Stella because I was standing there awkwardly trying to figure out what to say next. I didn't know the extent of whatever Christian told them about me but it seemed like his mother had already made up her mind about me. When Stella came over to introduce herself it gave us all a chance to break things up.

"Hello Mr. and Mrs. Harper," she said as she walked over to us. "I am Dr. Stella Fraiser, one of the attending doctors here. I just want you to know that we're taking good care of this one. Christian is a part of our family and we don't plan on letting him, or you, down."

Mrs. Harper looked Stella up and down and though she didn't say it outright, I could tell that she approved of her more than me. "I appreciate that," she said.

"It's the truth. Christian's is a face that we're used to seeing around here. The entire hospital is praying for him." Stella said with a solemn smile. "Dr. Jameson and I were just about to head out. Why don't we leave the two of you alone with your son? We've intruded long enough."

"Thank you," Mr. Harper said. "It was nice meeting the both of you. We hope to see you again." He offered up a kind smile which Stella and I both returned.

Stella and I left the room and headed down the hall a little bit. Once we were far enough away from the room, she started speaking to me in a hushed tone.

"So what did you think of Mr. and Mrs. Harper?" Stella asked me. "He's nice but she's something else." She chuckled.

"They were...interesting," I said. "Very interesting, that's for sure."

"They're nice people," she responded. "I've met them once or twice. They run in the same circles as my parents. Mrs. Harper can come across a certain kind of way, but she has a good heart. She donates a lot of money to a lot of charities."

"Oh, ok. High society types," I answered.

Stella looked troubled for a few seconds before sighing and then speaking. "So it looks like Christian took you more seriously than you thought," she acknowledged. "Did you know he told his parents about you?"

"No. I wasn't expecting any of that," I said with a casual shake of my head. The more I thought about it, the more confused I became. I didn't understand how Christian could be so serious as to tell his parents about me and him but at the same time threaten Miles over me and my job. It was like there were two different sides to him. I was wrestling with my thoughts, but I wasn't about to let Stella in on any of that.

"I don't wanna get up in your business or anything again, but I think you really should take some time to really get to know Christian," Stella prompted. "I know we've talked about this before, but it seems like Christian is, or at least was, really committed to you. We both know how Christian could be and I don't peg him as the type to tell his parents about all of his escapades. If he mentioned you, it's probably because he thinks you're special."

"You could be right," I said. I was trying to just listen and keep my opinions to myself. I wasn't trying to dismiss what she was saying, but if she knew the entire story, she'd probably be telling me otherwise. I wasn't going to inform her though.

"I don't know what's happening with you and Miles and I'm not saying any of this to try and piss you off, but he's dangerous. It's just a fact. I'm just trying to offer up my best advice. You know I want what's best for you. That's all I've ever wanted," Stella went on.

"Thanks," I said through almost gritted teeth. I was working hard to keep my emotions in check. On top of all the other shit that I was dealing with, I didn't want to deal with Stella on top of it all.

"I'm not mad," I lied. I thought for a minute or two that Stella might be cool again, but we were one conversation in and she was already trashing Miles again. I couldn't' believe it. She was like a dog with a bone. "I'm gonna think about what you're saying. Right now I'm just focused on helping Christian get better so he can get out of here."

"I feel you on that. It kind of makes you think about life when things like this happen," she shot back. "Look, I'm about to head to another room. I've got a follow up with some-one. I'll check in with you a little later in the day."

"See you," I called after her as she headed down the hall. As much as I hated to admit it, maybe there was some truth to what Stella was saying. I at least owed it to myself to look into Christian and his feelings for me. I wanted to know what else he'd been saying about me.

**CHAPTER 15**

S tella and I ended up meeting up with one another a little later on in the day. Since I'd come in that morning, I'd been thinking about Christian and his care. I voiced my concerns to her that we might be overdoing it with the medication and told her that I believed it was time for us to start to get him off of it. Much to my surprise, she agreed with me. She put in the request for the amount of medication that he was getting to be lowered significantly. He should have been waking up sometime in the next few hours.

With that in mind, I decided to stick around after my shift ended. I knew that I could have gone back to my house and dealt with Miles, who'd let me know that he hadn't left, but I wanted to be there in case Christian woke up. I felt like it would be best for him to wake up to seeing a familiar face as opposed to being alone. I'd had a lot of patients tell me about waking up from surgeries or other things that they needed to be asleep for, and how the disorientation of it all could be a lot.

I walked into the chilly room that Christian was in. It was evening time. The pink and orange skies shined bright through the window in his high up room. I looked at his bedside and saw that someone had left him some flowers and balloons. I assumed they were from his parents or some other family member.

I plopped down in the chair next to his bed. The chair was starting to feel more comfortable than it had before. I guessed that all my nights of sleeping there had left it with a permanent groove just for me.

Miles was on my mind still. At times it didn't even feel like I thought about myself. I was always worried about someone else and their wellbeing. Seeing the police earlier in Christian's room and knowing that they were now involved hadn't done anything to put my mind at ease. I knew that Miles had told me over and over again not to worry about anything but what was I supposed to do? It seemed like things were coming to a head, slowly but surely. Christian was set to wake up and the police made it clear that they'd be back to ask more questions when he got up.

My mind was still battling over everything that I'd learned. I couldn't believe that Christian had been out here threatening me and my job. I knew that Miles wouldn't lie about something like that. As I looked down at Christian, I saw that some of the color was coming back to his face. I studied him, wondering what had been going through his mind in the moments before he got shot. Had he been serious about his threats? What would happen once he woke up?

"Kal... Kallie," a hoarse voice croaked out a sound. I wasn't even sure if it was my name at first. It snapped me from my thoughts. I looked up at Christian and saw that his eyes were open. His head was slightly turned towards me.

"Oh my God!" I exclaimed. I stood up and moved closer to the bed. "Christian, you're awake."

His eyes were very much alert, even if it

looked like the rest of him would still need more time to recover. His eyes darted around the room taking it all in before he finally fixed his gaze on me. I could see from the frantic look in them that he was frightened and confused.

"Wa…" He tried to speak but coughed. "Water."

"I should've known," I said. I ran out of the room and down the hall towards the ice machine. I grabbed a cup and filled it with water and grabbed a second one just in case. I knew how dry his throat would be.

I headed back into the room and held each of them up to his mouth to help him swallow them down. He didn't thank me, but I could tell that he felt relieved after he finished them.

I gave Christian a few minutes to get himself centered again. It was almost like watching someone being born again. He asked for more water. I brought it to him and he drank it down quickly as he did before. I watched as he started to try out different parts of his body. Relief washed over him when he realized that while he was in pain, everything still seemed to work fine. Once he seemed like he was finished he turned his attention back to me.

"I'm glad you're here," he said. He stifled a yawn. "I'm so tired."

"I can imagine. You still have a lot of the medicine inside of you," I responded. I sat back down in the chair and scooted it a little closer to his bedside. Christian reached out for my hand. I took it in his. "I'm glad you're awake."

"Me too," he agreed. "I don't know how long I was out, but I feel like I could sleep for a few more days."

I didn't even realize how tired I was, but somehow, I ended up falling asleep right there in the chair, still hand in hand with Christian. I woke up a few hours later, startled and confused. It took me a couple of seconds to remember where I was and who I was with. I looked over at Christian who'd fallen back to sleep. I didn't want to wake him, so I gently let his hand go and got up to leave.

I was almost away from the bed when I felt his hand grab my finger. I turned to see that he was waking back up, or maybe he'd never been asleep in the first place.

"Stay," he said. He tried to sit up a little bit in the bed but his strength was low. "Please."

I turned back to face him. "I would, but I

can't." I looked down at my watch. "It's getting late and I still have work in the morning. But I'll be back first thing, alright?"

It seemed like some of the old Christian was coming back. He tried to sit himself up a little bit more, this time using the rails on the side of the bed to help him. The look on his face had become more serious as well. If I didn't know any better, I'd assume he was upset about something.

"Kallie, I just woke up. You must have been waiting for me to get up. I don't know why you can't just stay," Christian said. His voice was even sounding almost the same as before, just a little weaker. He still spoke in a way that made it sound like he was delivering orders and not making a request.

I was trying to keep him calm. There was no point in upsetting him so much when he'd just woken up. I walked back over to the bed. "I was waiting for you to get up, but you still need your rest. I can stop by and see you tomorrow. You don't know it, but I was by your bedside this whole time." I smiled at him in an attempt to make him feel better. I thought what I was doing was nice but then I realized that he wasn't smiling back at me.

"Why do you need to leave? I just woke up and you can't even stay here with me?" Christian asked. "You need to go see your drug dealing boyfriend? That must be it."

The more things change, the more they stayed the same. I kept my face blank as I listened to his question, but I couldn't believe it. He'd been in a medically induced coma for a while and had only been up for a few hours, but somehow he'd already let his mind go back to a jealous place. Men were something else. I clearly couldn't deal with him in a rational way. I decided not to answer him.

Christian was staring up at me from his hospital bed and the look on his face was one of anger. I didn't know what was going through his mind, but it couldn't have been anything good.

"Kallie…" Christian called to me and there was something behind his voice that I couldn't put my finger one. "Why can't you just stay?"

I took a deep breath and let it out slowly. "Christian, I have things to do. Like I said, I'll be back to see you tomorrow." I turned and headed towards the door.

"Go ahead then," Christian called back to me, "go back to the man who shot me."

I stopped dead in my tracks. I turned around and studied his face to make sure that I'd heard him right. Christian was looking smug with a smirk on his face. He seemed to be getting pleasure from having just spooked me.

"What... what are you talking about?" I took a couple of steps towards the bed until I was at the foot of it. "Who shot you? If you remember, you should tell the police."

"You're not a good liar," Christian said. "Never have been and apparently never will be."

"Christian, I—"

"No, you don't speak right now, you listen," he said. His voice had gotten a little louder than it was before. His entire mood seemed to darken in that moment. "Cause if you wanna keep your little boyfriend out of jail, things are gonna change. You've been running around out of control for too long but I'm awake now and if you want me to keep quiet, you're gonna keep me happy by doing what I tell you to do."

I was staring Christian right in his face but for the life of me, it felt like I couldn't recognize him. Was he actually trying to blackmail me? I couldn't believe it, but it seemed like that's what he was getting at. I couldn't even deny knowing about him and Miles because it was clear that he knew that I knew.

"Why would you even wanna do something like this? What do you want from me?" I asked him. I folded my arms across my chest in order to look more tough. It was the only thing I could do since he was the one holding all the cards.

"I think we both know why," he said. He looked my body up and down with his eyes. "I let you make your own choices before and look where it got me. No more of that. You need to make a choice, Kallie, and I think you already know what it needs to be."

My mind was racing to try and find an angle to work or something to say. I could feel my hands starting to get clammy with sweat. "If you really believe that Miles shot you, why not just got to the cops? He should have his day in court same as anyone else. You know the police would believe you."

Christian sighed. "We both know what kind of man he is," he explained. "If I went to the cops and it looked like there was a chance he'd end up in jail, I think we both know that I'd end up in the morgue long before that happened."

I focused my eyes on him but didn't say anything. I would have loved the chance to argue against it, but he was right. Miles had connections and could work the police and stuff because he paid a lot of them. The easiest way to make a case go away though was to get rid of any proof of a crime. If there were no witnesses, who'd be able to say anything to him?

"So in order for me to have some insurance, I'm letting you know that *I* know," Christian stated. "You're my insurance cause I know nothing's gonna happen to me. Just like I know you're gonna run back and tell him everything I just told you."

I shook my head. "Why are you doing all this? What did I ever do to you for you to want to hurt me like this?" I wracked my brain trying to grasp it but it didn't work. It was like I was finding out who Christian was all over again.

"Oh please." He rolled his eyes at me. "Don't stand there acting like you didn't do anything wrong. You played me, Kallie. You made me believe we had a future and then you decided to get with some drug dealer. I could have made you my wife!"

"Christian, I never meant to—"

"Never meant to what? Make me look like a fool? Well you did! But it's alright. I have to treat this like business and I always do well in business."

"What does that even mean?" I asked, curiously. Christian wasn't talking like anyone that I knew. If I would have known that he'd wake up and start acting so crazy, I definitely would have recommended that his ass stayed asleep.

"You'll find out," he replied in a cold tone. "But you might wanna think about leaving the drug dealer alone if you know what's good for you."

## CHAPTER 16

I couldn't get out of the hospital fast enough. My conversation with Christian had me shook to my core. It was like something out of a soap opera. I couldn't believe that he'd woken up and had immediately become so vindictive. It wasn't that I didn't believe he was capable of it; he'd more than proven that in the last few days with his actions regarding Miles. I was just surprised that having almost died hadn't really done anything to make him see the error of his ways. If anything, he seemed even *more* determined to make trouble for everyone.

When I got home I called out to Miles, but he wasn't there. I put my bag down on the counter and headed over to the dinner table. I opened the door that led to my balcony and let some fresh air in. It felt like the walls were closing in on me. I was so filled with worry. I pulled out my phone to call Miles but as luck would have it, he was using his key at that exact same moment to let himself back in.

He walked into the apartment carrying a large box of pizza. He smiled when he saw me and started heading my way.

"I got some pizza," he said as he made his way over to me, "I figured you'd be too tired for anything else." Miles set the pizza box down on the table as he looked at my face. He must have finally seen the worry in my eyes. "What's wrong?"

I stood up and started pacing. "Christian woke up. He's talking crazy. I can't believe him. What are we gonna do? He remembers everything. I can't do this, I—"

"Kallie, relax," Miles said in a calming way. He walked around the table towards me and put his hands on my shoulders. He kissed me on the forehead and then pulled me in for a tight hug. "Yo, just breathe. Take some deep breaths and then tell me what happened."

The closeness of Miles to me was calming me down. I did as he said as I inhaled and exhaled deeply. I pulled myself away from him and looked him in the eyes so that he knew I was being serious.

"I think you should sit down for this," I suggested to him.

Miles folded his arms across his chest defiantly. "Nah, I'm good," he said with a shake of his head. "What happened?"

I went ahead and took a seat. "Like I said, Christian is awake. He's made it clear to me that he remembers everything that happened, including the fact that you were the person who shot him."

Miles nodded his head in understanding. "That's nothing we didn't expect. I mean, I definitely wish that he ain't remember anything, but we knew there was a chance that he'd have his memories."

"That's not all," I went on. "He threatened us. He didn't come right out and say it, but he made it clear that he wants us to break up or else he's gonna tell the police what happened."

Miles slammed his hand down on the table hard, causing it to shake. "That dirty motherfucker!" He growled with anger. "I can't believe he's got the nerve to try some shit like this."

"Miles, try and calm down," I said.

"Hell no!" Miles snapped. "I could've killed that nigga! You saved his life! I can't believe he woke up and got right back on this bullshit. I want that nigga dead."

I shook my head. "Miles, you're talking crazy. You can't do nothing to him and you know it."

"What do you mean I can't do anything to him?" Miles asked.

I let out a sigh. "Look, unless you're about to march up to the hospital and get him right now before the police have a chance to question him, you're out of options. Even if you did go, do you really think you'd be able to get in and out of his room without anyone seeing you? I know you're angry but hurting Christian...or anything worse, isn't really an option on the table."

Miles' big, muscular chest heaved up and down as he listened to me. Finally, he let out his breath and took a seat the table. His jaw was clenched and his hands were balled up into fists, but at least he'd calmed down some.

"This is some bullshit," Miles said.

I couldn't help but to nod my head. "I hope it wasn't a trap or something."

"What you mean?" Miles asked in confusion.

"I never came out and said directly that I knew anything about you shooting him, but what if Christian was trying to record me or something? I know it's a little out there but at this point I think it's probably best if we don't take anything off the table."

"I think you're being paranoid," Miles countered. "I know he's crazy and all but he wouldn't record you or anything, not when all the police need is his testimony. With all his money and power plus my record, he'd be fine and I'd be locked up."

"Maybe we shouldn't be together," I blurted out. Miles looked at me as he heard the words. I'd been thinking about it on the way home as I wracked my brain trying to find a solution to our problems.

It wasn't like Christian was the type of person who would just go away. I would see him around the hospital regardless of what happened. He couldn't be paid off, partially because Miles didn't have that kind of money, but also because he wasn't out for anything other than revenge. He was hurt and wanted to hurt everyone else that was involved as well.

My car ride home had given me lots of time to myself to think. I knew that Christian wouldn't be satisfied unless he knew that Miles and I weren't together. I couldn't even figure out if he wanted me for himself or if he just didn't want me with Miles. The more I thought about it, the more I realized that the only way to make the situation go away would be for me to do the thing that would probably make me the unhappiest: leave Miles.

"What makes you think that?" Miles asked. He reached out and grabbed my hand across the table. "Cause if you thought I was gonna say that I was cool with that, you got another thing coming."

"This wouldn't be easy for me," I said. "You know it's not something I want to do but if the alternative is Christian doing something to force us apart, I feel like we owe it to ourselves to at least explore the option."

Miles shook his head. "Nah, we can't do that. We can figure something out, we always do. I don't wanna lose you over this."

I wanted to say something else but couldn't find the words. It wasn't as though I was trying to hurt Miles; in fact, it was quite the opposite. I didn't expect for him to just give up without a fight but I'd at least been hoping that he'd be able to see things from my point of view before he shot them down. I felt like I had the weight of the world on my shoulders.

Miles and I sat in silence for a few minutes. It felt like the two of us had just run out of words. Our hands were still holding on to one another, but I could see that our minds were in different places. Every now and then I'd catch him sneaking a glance at me as if he we were trying to study me and find an answer.

"I can't... I won't...," Miles sighed as he broke the silence, trying to gather his thoughts and piece them together. "I won't sit here and lie to you and say that I don't want us to be together. But I can see how much this is hurting you and for that reason, I'm just gonna go with whatever you choose to do."

"Miles, that means a lot to me," I said as I squeezed his hand.

"I don't want you to feel like you're being held hostage or anything like that. I know you're just trying to keep the peace," he went on. "All I ask is that you give me a little more time to try and fix my own mess."

I nodded my head. "No problem. I really appreciate you for going through with this. I'm not a hundred percent about anything yet though so don't go running out on me," I tried to joke with him and lighten the mood.

"Nah, never that," Miles responded with a weak smile.

After our talk, Miles and I tried to act as normal as possible. We ate the pizza he'd brought and watched some TV. It all felt a little awkward though because it almost felt a little forced. I knew that the two of us were both still very much in our heads about everything that was happening.

Thankfully Miles ended up staying the night again. Having his arms around me was comforting but it wasn't helping me go to sleep. I'd been tossing and turning for the better part of two hours and it didn't look like I was going to head off into dreamland any time soon. I looked at Miles, who seemed to be sleeping like a baby. I ended up having to get up and drink a glass of chamomile tea before I was finally able to head to sleep.

I'd been hoping that my sleep would bring me some peace and relaxation, but it didn't work out that way at all. I ended up having a dream about Miles and Christian.

*I was somehow at the hospital again, back in Christian's room. I was in the room but it didn't seem like he could see or hear me. I was standing in front of the window watching Christian on his phone. He was texting someone, but I couldn't tell who.*

*The door to the hospital room had been closed but somehow it burst open. Miles came in, but in my dream he appeared to be bigger and stronger than he normally was. He rounded the corner and stood at the foot of Christian's bed. Christian put his phone down and looked up at Miles with a smug look on his face.*

*"I thought I'd be seeing you soon," Christian said to Miles. Much to my surprise, he got up out of the bed and was somehow dressed in normal clothing instead of a hospital gown.*

*"You pulled some bullshit with Kallie," Miles exclaimed. "You had to know that I was gonna come for you."*

*"So what do you think you're about to do to me?" Christian asked. Maybe it was because it was my dream*

*and I knew what was going on, but I could tell that Miles wasn't picking up on any of the clues that were being dropped on him.*

*"What I should've done before," Miles responded. He reached into his pants and pulled out a gun. I felt the fear rise up in me. He pointed it squarely at Christian and even took a couple of steps towards him in a threatening manner.*

*"Oh, you mean shooting me the first time wasn't enough?" Christian shot back. He raised his hands in apparent fear but there was still something off about the entire thing.*

*"I should've killed your ass then. I would have if I'd have known you were gonna cause this much trouble."*

*"That's all I needed to hear," a voice said. The door to the room hadn't opened up again but somehow it was filled up with police officers. They all had their guns pointed at Miles. Miles put his hands up in the air.*

*The dream changed to a different setting. We were in a courtroom now. It was filled to the brim with people. I looked down at myself to see that I was now dressed in an all-black pantsuit. I moved slowly to the bench behind the defendants and looked up to see that it was Miles.*

*There was a judge at the front of the large room. It was tough to make out what the person looked like. It might have been a man in his late 40s. Either way, for as unclear as what the person looked like was, the voice was just as clear. It was deep and foreboding as it dished out its justice.*

*"Miles Johnson," the voice boomed, "please rise."*

*Miles was sitting right in front of me, alone, no lawyer or anything. I stood up when he did. I turned my head and saw Christian on the other side of the courtroom. He was wearing a devilish grin on his face.*

*"For the charges of attempted murder and drug trafficking, you are hereby sentenced to life in prison without the possibility of parole!" The voice condemned Miles.*

*I let out a yell in the dream as two bailiffs appeared and grabbed Miles. They were on both sides of him as they led him towards a side door. He turned his head towards me and smiled sadly before they took him out the door.*

*I was filled with the feeling that I would never see him again. The feeling was so strong that it actually woke me up out of my sleep.*

I sat up and took a couple of deep breaths. It felt like I'd been gasping for air. I turned my head and saw that Miles was still sleeping soundlessly next to me, unaware of what I was going through.

I lowered myself back into the bed slowly. Looking over at the clock, I saw that I'd been asleep for a little over two hours. It didn't even feel like it. I almost felt *more* tired than I had when I'd gone to sleep.

I knew that my dream had come from my own fears. I knew that I was regretting the fact that I'd told Miles everything but there wasn't another option for me. There was definitely every chance that he'd go back to Christian and do something stupid, but I didn't believe that he would. It was at the point where things could spiral out of control if we weren't careful and I needed to stop trying to do it all alone.

As I cuddled up to Miles, I thought about Christian and his warning to me. I knew that he wanted me for himself and at a minimum, he wanted me away from Miles. This was going to be one of the hardest decisions that I ever had to make.

## CHAPTER 17

Miles and I got up to leave the following morning around the same time. He asked me how I'd slept and I lied to him, saying that I'd gotten a good night's sleep. I'd been able to get back to sleep, but I wouldn't call what I did restful.

I headed into work and started my rounds. I checked my schedule and saw that Christian was one of the people I'd have to see during my rotation. I was dreading seeing him, knowing that he was only going to keep going with his plan to ruin my life.

I put it off for as long I could. I tried to stall all the patients that I was working with so that I could hold out on seeing Christian. Unfortunately, it turned out to be one of those days where everything was pretty straightforward. No one gave me any trouble and none of the patients seemed to have much in the way of conversation wither.

I made my way to the floor that Christian was on. It was almost funny because I'd been spending so much time there when he was asleep but now that he'd woken up, it was the last place I wanted to be. I turned the corner and headed into the room, surprised to see his parents standing over his bed. I didn't want to turn on the fakeness, but I couldn't be as direct with Christian as I wanted to. Not with his parents there at least.

The presence of his parents had put a wrench in my plans. My intentions were to speak to Christian to try and get him to call the whole thing off If I couldn't do that, I'd at least try and get more time out of him so that I could make up my mind.

"Good afternoon," I said as I knocked on the door. I plastered a fake smile on my face. Mr. Harper returned it. It looked like Mrs. Harper was trying to smile, but in reality, it came across like she'd smelled something that stank.

"Dr. Jameson, nice to see you again," Mr. Harper said.

"Nice to see you both as well," I said. I walked a little closer to the bed and grabbed Christian's chart. Looking down at it I saw that all of his numbers were in the range that they should have been in. I moved closer to Christian's bedside and when I did, he grabbed me by the hand. I was trying to resist him but with his parents there, I had no other choice but to comply. He pulled me closer to him until I was low enough for him to kiss me full on the lips.

We broke the kiss and I whispered to Christian that I hadn't made any choices about anything yet. His eyes momentarily narrowed at me, but he didn't say anything else.

"Oh?" Mrs. Harper said in mock surprise. "Are you two getting back together?"

"Who knows? The choice is up to my little doctor right here," Christian said. He patted my hand condescendingly. "But she's been here for me day in and day out, so I wanted to thank her properly."

"We'll see what the future holds," I

commented. "For right now, my biggest concern is making sure that Miles gets out of this hospital."

His parents might not have been picking up on what I was saying but Christian for sure knew what my message to him was. I was making it clear that I had no intention on getting back with him.

I was standing there feeling awkward and uncomfortable as Christian put on his little show for his parents. I smiled in a fake way as he talked. He had some fucking nerve pulling a stunt like this, especially in front of visitors.

We were about to continue our conversation when a knock at the door interrupted us. We all turned around at about the same time. The two detectives that had come before when Christian was still sleeping had returned. They had smiles on their faces this time.

"Mr. Harper, we heard you were awake so we wanted to come and talk to you if that's alright," said the Latino detective from before. "I'm Detective Ramos and this is Detective Herald. We're the ones assigned to your case."

Fear rose up inside of me. I was trying my best to hide it but when I looked down at Christian and the smug smirk on his face, it did nothing to calm me down. It was obvious that Christian was a fan of their timing. It couldn't have come at a better time for him than it did.

Christian nodded at them. "I can give you guys a few minutes now," he said.

"That sounds good," said Detective Herald. He looked at Christian's parents and me. "Would you all be able to give us the room?"

Mr. and Mrs. Harper nodded and began to exit the room slowly. I was in panic mode, at least on the inside. I'd told Christian moments before that I hadn't made a decision about being with him. If he carried his annoyance and anger at that into his conversation with the police, Miles and I could both end up going down.

I stood firmly where I was. "I was actually just starting my rounds on him," I said. "I want to be able to finish it so I can move on to the next patient."

The cops looked at one another and then back at me. "Dr...?"

"Dr. Jameson," I said.

"Dr. Jameson, it's really important that we talk to Mr. Harper right now," said Detective

Ramos. "Would you be able to come back in a little bit?"

"I really want to finish this right now," I countered. "Trust, it won't take that long."

"Ma'am, I'm afraid we're gonna have to insist," he shot back.

"Kallie, just step outside. I'll be fine," Christian finally chimed in. I looked at him with annoyance on my face. I wanted to put up more of a fight but I knew that it would look suspicious if I did.

"You're right," I responded, "but, I'll be back in ten minutes. I need to finish this up. Christian is due to get some more medicine and it needs to be taken on a strict time schedule." I was lying. Christian did need to have some more medicine administered but it wasn't a pressing issue, nor was it something that was on a strict schedule. As long as he took it that day he'd be fine.

"Not a problem," said Detective Herald.

I headed outside of the room to wait with Mr. and Mrs. Harper. The door was still open so I was sure that I'd be able to hear whatever they were saying inside.

"So... Dr. Jameson," said Mr. Harper as he

grabbed my attention. I turned to face him, staring at his handsome and older face.

"You can call me Kallie," I said in a friendly way. "After all, I did date your son."

"Alright, Kallie," Mr. Harper said with a smile. He wasn't even doing anything at all but the man was incredibly charming. "So, how do things look for Christian?"

"He should be fine. I mean, he was pretty banged up, but he shouldn't need to be in here much longer," I explained.

Mrs. Harper, who was sitting down on a chair outside the room, stood up and made her way over to us. She was edging slowly towards us as though she wasn't sure if she could approach.

"My husband isn't as direct as I am," she interjected, "so I'll cut right to the point. Have you given any thought to what's going to happen between you and our son?"

Mr. Harper shot his wife a warning look but didn't open his mouth to silence her. I felt awkward with the two of them standing there staring at me.

"I... uh…. I hadn't really given it much thought," I said nervously. I regained some of my usual confidence soon after. "Honestly, I'm just focused on making sure that Christian receives the best care possible. Anything outside of that is on hold for right now."

Mr. Harper smiled and nodded, apparently pleased with my answer. Mrs. Harper was studying my face.

"You know, when my son first told me about you, I was a little skeptical," she said. "I mean, and this isn't meant to offend you, but I had an issue with your upbringing."

"My upbringing?" I asked in confusion and annoyance.

"Please, don't judge me too harshly," Mrs. Harper said. She held up her hands to show she meant no harm. "I just want what's best for my son, same as any other mother would. Christian made it clear to me that while you might have been raised on the... Southside," she said the word with disgust as it left her mouth, "you've put all of that behind you. He's also made it clear that if he had a choice, he'd choose you."

I would have been flattered or felt something more in regard to what Mrs. Harper said but I was distracted. I could hear that the police were finally done with the introduction of the facts and were starting to get to the question and answer portion.

"Well, Christian and I apparently have some things to talk about," I said with a smile. I took a couple of small steps back so that I could hear a little better.

*"So, Mr. Harper, what do you remember about the events of the day you were shot?"* I could hear Detective Ramos starting to interview Christian. My heart was speeding up and I felt more nervous than ever. *"Try to recall them as best you can. You may not remember everything in order but whatever information you can give us would be helpful.'*

It got silent for a moment and then I heard Christian sigh. *"Well, I was driving. I'd pulled over for something, but I can't remember what. I got out of the car and—"*

*"Why'd you get out of the car?"* Detective Herald asked.

*"I think I thought something was wrong with it,"* Christian went on. *"Yeah, that's why I pulled over. The car was making noises and I pulled over to see if I could figure out what was wrong with it."*

*"Alright, go on,"* Detective Ramos urged.

*"It all gets kind of cloudy from there,"* Christian

*went on. "I don't have it all but I remember flashes of things... images and feelings, if that makes any sense."*

*"Whatever you can remember is helpful," said Detective Herald.*

"Kallie, are you alright?" Mr. Harper's deep voice snapped me from my thoughts.

"Huh? What'd you say?" I asked. If he'd been talking to me I didn't know. I was too busy listening to the conversation inside the room.

"I asked if you were alright," he repeated.

I shook my head a little in an effort to play it off. "I'm just worried about Christian," I lied. "It's a lot for him to go through."

"I can see you really care about him," Mrs. Harper said. She seemed to warm up to me a little bit after that.

*"Were you able to get a look at who shot you?" Detective Ramos asked*

*"I think I did," Christian said. He was putting on quite a performance. It almost sounded like he'd conjured up some emotion or something. "I think I can describe him and probably point him out. As a matter of fact, I think I know who it was."*

*"Who?"*

*"My girlfriend's ex-boyfriend," Christian stated.*

At that moment I'd heard more than

enough. I was seething and needed to break up their conversation before it went further. I turned and headed back into the room. I walked loudly, my heels clicking and clacking on the floor.

"Well gentlemen, it's time for Christian to get his antibiotics. He's still at a great risk of infection," I said loudly. I grabbed Christian's chart and looked at the two detectives expectantly.

"Doctor, we're in the middle of an interview," Detective Herald protested.

"Well, you're also in the middle of a hospital, and he's a victim, not a suspect. I have a job to do as well," I retorted. I went into a drawer on the other side of the room with medical supplies and grabbed the bag of medicine that I needed.

"We can wait," Detective Ramos said.

I turned my back to the detectives as I changed out the medicine bag. Inside I was losing it. I looked at my hands and saw that they were shaking. It had to be out of fear and anger. I couldn't believe Christian was about to force my hand that way.

The police went on with the interview.

"So Mr. Harper, you mentioned a girlfriend and an ex of hers?" Detective Ramos went on.

"Well, you might as well ask her yourself, since it's Dr. Jameson here," Christian said. I could hear the smugness in his voice. I finished with the bag of medicine and turned back around. The eyes of all three of the men in the room were on me.

I was even more surprised than before. I didn't believe that Christian would put me on the spot the way that he did. It was clear that he was getting some kind of sick pleasure from it.

"Dr. Jameson," Detective Ramos was looking at me with confusion, "you never said that you were his girlfriend."

I responded, "Christian and I have been in a kind of on again, off again thing for the last few months."

The two detectives exchanged a look with one another. "So, who is this ex-boyfriend of yours? Mr. Harper seems to be under the assumption that he might have had something to do with his shooting."

I was being an actress at that point. I looked at Christian with surprise and confusion and then back at the police. "Really? I don't know what would make him think something like that. My ex isn't really that type of guy."

Detective Ramos was intent on not dropping the point. "Well, Mr. Harper seems to be really convinced. Do you have any idea why that might be?"

I nodded my head. "Well, he and my ex engaged in some back and forth before, but it wasn't anything more than jealousy. I haven't heard from my ex in months. Honestly, the last I'd heard of him, he'd moved out of the state and was seeing someone else."

"Out of the state, huh?" Detective Herald was clearly skeptical of my answer.

I nodded to reaffirm my point. "Yes," I said. "I told Christian about that, but he's just the jealous type."

"Well, maybe we should get his name just to check that out," Detective Ramos said.

My heart was pounding in my chest as I turned towards Christian. He smiled at me and then looked at the cops.

"Actually officers, I believe I might be wrong," he said.

Detective Ramos' eyes scanned me and then narrowed at Christian. "Wrong? Really?"

Christian nodded his head. "Yeah, now that I think about it, I could be getting it all messed up. It's still a little cloudy in my head. It was probably just some scum from the Southside who'd been following me."

"What makes you think that?"

"I mean, who else would it be? They probably spotted me coming out of work and saw that I looked like I had money," he explained. Christian reached out and grabbed my hand, pulling it closer to him and kissing it.

The two detectives didn't look like they were sold on the explanation that they'd been given. They shared another glance with each other before turning back to us.

Detective Ramos took a couple of steps towards us. He reached into his jacket pocket and pulled out two business cards.

"We'll have more questions, but we should probably get going, at least for right now," he said. "If *either* of you remember anything else, give us a call."

"We definitely will. Won't we, *baby?*" Christian patted my hand and looked up at me. He was eating it up.

"Yep," I chimed in.

The two detectives turned and left the room. Once I was sure they were gone I snatched my hand away from Christian and turned to him with fury in my eyes.

"What the hell is wrong with you? Telling them I'm your girlfriend? That's not a part of the deal! If you want me to leave Miles alone then that's one thing," I fumed.

Christian shrugged his shoulders. "You'll come around eventually. Either way, I'm just glad that the gang banger is out of the way."

"Whatever," I growled.

"And don't think about sneaking around to get with him or anything like that," Christian said. "For one thing, I'll find out. Beyond that, I think we both know the cops are more confused than ever about what happened. I've already planted a seed of doubt in their heads. If I have to go back and water it, I will."

"You're sick, you know that?" I was on the verge of breaking down. It felt like the walls were closing in around me. I knew that in order to protect Miles, I might have to leave him. The reality of the situation was finally washing over me. In those last few moments with Christian and the police in his room, I'd made my choice.

It hadn't been the way that I wanted it to go, but Christian was working against me, so it forced me to act.

I didn't say anything else to Christian. I was on the verge of yelling and screaming, not only at him but the entire situation. I wanted to be far away. I walked quickly, almost breaking into a run at one point. I walked past Christian's parents and ignored them calling out to me.

"Kallie, wait up," a voice said from behind me. I turned to see that Stella had been following me. She had been trying to be friend-lier towards me recently, so I stopped moving and turned to face her.

Stella and I were nowhere close to being friends on the level that we were at before. I didn't feel comfortable enough with her to share the full extent of what was happening. I made something up instead.

"It's just stuff with Christian," I said.

"What's he doing?" she pressed. She was trying to be a friend and it was welcome, even if I couldn't be totally honest with her.

"He's just putting pressure on me in front of his parents," I said. "I already told him how I feel about that, so I don't know why he keeps pressing me."

"You're strong," Stella comforted me, "and you know how to navigate a situation. Don't let yourself feel overwhelmed, especially not by Christian. He's never been able to push you around."

I thanked her for her words and the two of us managed a hug. Her advice wasn't specific to my situation, but it was still greatly appreciated.

"I really needed that," I said.

## CHAPTER 18

Miles and I had been texting all day long. He usually texted me through the day, but lately he'd been even more on top of it than usual. I think it was the guilt that he'd been feeling, plus he knew how stressed out I was over everything with Christian so he was just looking out for me. I'd been answering him all day but I hadn't really had much to say.

I kept the conversation purely on the surface level. He asked how I was doing and I'd say I was alright without going into too many details. I didn't want to tip him off to anything being wrong. I couldn't tell him about the things that happened and the decision that I made via text; it would have to be in person.

I ended up going to lunch right after meeting with Christian and the police. It felt like I couldn't get out of the hospital fast enough. Stella offered to go with me but I told her that I just wanted some time to myself. She didn't seem offended or anything and I was glad that she'd at least offered. It seemed to be a step in the right direction for our friendship.

Having the time to myself on my lunch break really seemed to be helping me out. It was only an hour but being away from the hospital and the source of my stress was helping me out. I got to the deli and ordered a sandwich. Once it was done I headed upstairs to their small dining area and grabbed a table close to a window.

I sighed as I pulled out my phone to text Miles. I'd finally figured out how I wanted to handle the situation. I held the phone in my hand for a few minutes, trying to work up the nerve.

*Hey,* I sent the text to Miles. *What are you up to?"*

The response came back almost immediately. *Wassup? Chillin, you?*

*At work of course. What are you doing later on like around 8? I want you to meet me somewhere.*

*Ok, where at? You OK?* Miles' responses came through quickly. He really must not have been busy with anything.

On one of our first dates, Miles had taken me down to the harbor after dinner. We'd figured out that a certain spot on Lake Michigan was ours because we'd sat down on the dock and talked until the same came up. I figured that if I was going to drop a bombshell on him that it would probably be better to do it in a location familiar to us. I told him where I wanted to meet and when he asked why, I just told him that it was important. It was also important for me to meet Miles somewhere neutral. I knew that he wouldn't like what I had to say so it was probably better to be in public.

Miles agreed to meet me with no problems. That was the easy part, but I'd always known that it would be. It would be harder to break his heart in person later on that evening.

I knew that Miles would probably try and convince me otherwise later on, but I could only see how this was my fault. I felt like it was my mistakes that everyone else was paying for. If only I'd been more careful about how I'd handled things, then no one would be in the situation that they were in.

I shouldn't have started messing with Christian in the first place. He had too many skeletons in his closet and too many bodies to bury. I was setting myself up for trouble. I saw a lot of things in him that I didn't like in him and I decided to stay. I should have either kept it very casual with him or cut it off. The problem was that Christian was charming and for a hot second it seemed like things between us would work out. I was wrong though. Christian wasn't someone that I was supposed to take seriously.

My situation with Miles wouldn't have been half as complicated without Christian around. Miles wouldn't have had anyone to direct his jealousy towards. Don't get me wrong, I know that Miles and I would still have our own problems to deal with, but the added pressure of Christian wouldn't have been a factor at least.

In the long run I just hoped that Miles would see that everything I did and everything I'm doing is being done to protect him. My hand was being forced and there was nothing I could really do about. I wasn't expecting him to just roll over and take it, but I wanted him to see that I was playing the long game. The only way that I'd be able to keep him out of jail was by breaking up with him for the benefit of Christian.

The rest of my shift went by quickly at work once I got back from my break. I was glad that I'd already seen Christian for the day and wouldn't have to deal with him again. He'd done more than piss me off earlier, he hurt me. I knew that he must have felt some level of hurt over me but the way that he was making it seem was as though I had cheated on him with Miles and that wasn't the case. Christian and I were on ice before things with Miles got too serious. We might have had some conversations while I was sleeping with Christian, but they were harmless.

When I got home it took me forever to figure out what to wear to meet Miles. I must've changed my clothes at least three times. I didn't want to be too sexy, but I also didn't want to be too serious. What kind of clothes does someone wear to end a relationship with a man they believed would be the love of their life? I finally decided to just keep it simple with a pair of black jeans and a black, sleeveless shirt.

About twenty minutes before we were supposed to meet, I texted Miles and told him that I was on my way. I headed down to my car and sat in it for a minute before I headed out. I was having second thoughts about doing this. I knew it was something that I had to do, but not something that I wanted.

I parked my car close to the harbor and made my way over the spot that we'd picked out. The harbor was surprisingly still full of life. The night air was warm and there were no clouds in the sky. Every now and then I'd get passed by a runner or a group of people headed somewhere. The scent of the lake air hit my nose as I made my way.

I spotted Miles before he saw me. He was turned to the side but I could see him dressed in his white jeans and navy blue and white polo shirt. As always, he looked good and was super clean. He finally spotted me and turned towards me, grinning like a fool. It only hurt me even more to see him smiling and then to know that I'd be the cause of that smile fading.

When he saw me, he tried to give me a hug and kiss, but I held up my hand to stop him.

"What's wrong?" he asked me. He was frowning and his eyebrows came together closer out of confusion.

"We should sit down," I suggested. I pointed to a bench closer to the water's edge. We made our way over to it and I took a seat.

"I don't wanna sit," he said. He sounded like a kid who knew they were about to be punished.

"Miles, please. Don't make this harder on me than it has to be," I pleaded. I looked up at him. He sighed and then took a seat. It wasn't cold but he shoved his hands into his pockets and stared straight ahead into the distance. He was already picking up the vibes that I was giving off.

I'd wracked my brain going over the many ways that I could have done it. I'd finally come up with one that would help get my point across without it being a problem

I reached into my purse and pulled out a small bag from a short that I'd shopped at. The bag was filled with jewelry, all the jewelry that Miles had given me throughout our relationship, including the diamond bracelet that he'd given me when we were in New York. Sticking out of the bag was an envelope addressed to Miles. He didn't reach for the bag, so I just put it down on his lap.

He broke his stare off with the nighttime and looked down at the bag before looking back up.

"What's that?" he asked.

I knew that I could break out into tears any second and I didn't want to make it harder on either of us by doing that. Instead I focused on getting my point across before I left.

"I... I couldn't sit here and tell you how I felt. It's all in the letter," I explained. "You know that I love you and I always will, but this is for the best. It's not that this is something that I want to do, but I've brought a lot of trouble into your life and I don't want that for either of us anymore. For where you're at in life and what you're trying to do, you can't be distracted. I know you have goals and stuff and now you have a clear path to them."

Much to my surprise, Miles laughed lightly. "You think you know everything," he said.

"What you mean?" I asked.

"Kallie, I don't know what you think I do all

day, but I'm not no bum nigga. I don't sit around not doing anything. I've been making my moves, even with all this bullshit with that nigga Christian going on," he explained.

"What are you talking about?"

"I'm done with the game," he announced proudly. He turned his head to me and as I studied his eyes, I could see how serious he was about it. There was a glint of something like passion in his eyes and it warmed me to my core to see it. "You know I couldn't just up and leave with no one in charge so I made sure that I picked the right person. I applied to school and got in. I'm going back for business."

"Miles, I'm so proud of you," I gushed. "I'm glad that you're taking steps to make yourself better. You know that's all I ever wanted for you, for either of us really."

"Yeah and I wouldn't be doing any of it if it wasn't for you," Miles said. He moved a little closer to me. His mood seemed to get darker before he spoke again. "I'm assuming you're taking that nigga Christian up on his offer." He stated it matter-of-factly.

I didn't say anything for a while before I went over what happened during the day. I explained how Christian was on the verge of telling and had made it clear to me that if he found out I was still messing with Miles that he'd turn him into the police. I was open and honest about how I felt. I let Miles know that while I was open to other options, I didn't really see any that would get us out of the situation we were in.

"I just don't feel like I had a choice in the moment. Everything was happening so fast that I couldn't really react. I just had to go with it," I explained.

"Thank you for protecting me," he said, "but I asked you to give me more time to figure things out."

I knew breaking this to Miles wouldn't be easy, but he was making it that much harder for me the more he asked for answers and argued back.

"I didn't have any time in that moment. I had to do what needed to be done. You asking for time was fine with me but then the police came in and I had to make a move or else things could have gone wrong," I explained. "My hands were tied."

It was Miles' turn to get quiet. He finally let out a loud sigh of defeat. "I love you, Kallie. I know I might not say it enough, but I do. You're the type of woman who I could see me spending my life with. You're smart, funny, and you got a good heart. I just wish things would have worked out differently between us. I could sit here and argue with you all night about what we should do but I know it wouldn't make a real difference. The shit would probably hurt worse."

I felt a cold feeling wash over me. It was one that I'd been dreading all day long. It was the feeling that Miles understood where I was coming from and was preparing to leave. I knew that ultimately it was what I wanted to happen, but as the reality of it covered me, I felt myself fill with sadness.

Miles stood up. "I got a new number," he said before he texted it to me from his old phone. "If you hit the old number after tonight you won't get a response. New lifestyle means new things. I'm always here for you if you need me." Miles paused and shook his head. "I was thinking about leaving the city. I'd still go to school here but that might be it. I can't stay in the same place that I was in now that I'm not in the game anymore."

"Where would you go?" I asked.

He shrugged. "I don't know. I could move to another part of the state and just come into the city for school or I could stay for a year and transfer my credits elsewhere. I haven't really planned it out yet."

I stood up as well. I walked closer to him and grabbed his hands in mine. "Miles, I'm proud of you, no matter what you decide to do, I know you're gonna be the best at it. You know that if I had a choice, I'd choose you every time, but it just wasn't in the cards for us."

"Can I hold you again?" he asked. I could see that he was emotional. He wasn't close to tears like I was but he was going through something in his head. I could see it in his eyes.

I nodded my head. "Of course," I said.

Miles pulled out his phone and started playing some soft music. He wrapped his arm around my waist and pulled me closer to him. Tears silently cascaded down my face as the two of us rocked back and forth. I closed my eyes for a bit and rested my head on his chest. I wanted to enjoy the moment.

When the song went off, Miles and I separated a little bit. He looked down at me and lowered his head towards mine for a kiss. His full lips slowly embraced mine and we stayed there, wrapped up in one another for what felt like forever. The kiss was the sweetest one that I'd ever gotten from him, probably because we both knew it was goodbye. When it was over, we each took a step back from one another.

Miles handed me back the bag of gifts but held onto the letter that I'd written him.

"This is all I need," he stated. "The rest is yours, always was and always will be."

He stood there awkwardly as if he wanted to stay more. Instead he just turned and left without saying anything else and without looking back. I watched him walk off for a little before turning and heading the opposite way.

## CHAPTER 19

I stepped out of my apartment and made my way down the hallway towards the elevator. I pressed the button for it and waited while I secured my phone in the armband I was wearing. I was headed out for a run. It felt like forever since the last time that I'd gone out to do it. I knew that I was going to enjoy it.

A few minutes later I'd left the building and was running along my usual route towards the park. The early morning sun was still rising over the city but there were more than a few people out and about. I felt myself working up a sweat as I reached my trail and headed down it. It was almost strange how normal it felt.

It had been two months since the last time that I'd spoken to Miles and even longer since that night we left one another at the harbor. It felt like a lifetime ago. We tried to keep in touch. We'd speak every now and then, but it always started to feel too close and too familiar which only complicated things. He would sometimes try and argue with me about the whole Christian thing, but I made it clear to him that I didn't want to risk it.

One day without me realizing it, Miles stopped calling. It happened probably a week or so after one random phone call. I was at home and checked my phone only to see that we hadn't spoken in some time. I was close to calling him but decided not to. Now, two months later, I could only assume that he'd moved on with his life. I kept that thought in my mind as I made moves to do the same with mine.

After breaking up with Miles I was a mess. He and I splitting up wasn't something that I'd wanted to happen and the circumstances surrounding it only made it feel that much worse. It would have been something different if he and I had just naturally drifted apart or something like that, but being forced apart because we had a crime to cover up was nothing I'd ever imagined I'd be a part of.

I had to sit down and have a few real conversations with myself about who I was and what I was capable of. I agonize over the fact that Miles had been a patient of mine at first. I also reflected on how I stayed with him despite knowing the lifestyle that he was living. It made me realize that while I still wouldn't consider myself to be a rule breaker per say, I at least knew that I was capable of it when the situation called for it.

The same way that I'd let myself get into a funk was the same way that I managed to get myself out of it. It got easier when Miles stopped calling. I knew I always had the option of not picking up the phone, but I just couldn't help it; I loved the man. Deep down I knew that I would always care about him, but I had to put those feelings away for focus on me. I'd been so upset that I stopped doing the things I enjoyed doing. I was trying to find my way back to them.

At first, I tried to throw myself into work as I usually did. It helped for a little while, but I soon realized that it didn't feel the same. Don't get me wrong, I loved my job and it still fulfilled me. But Miles had shown me that there was much more to life than just working. I needed to find balance.

I also couldn't fully commit to things at the hospital because of Christian. He got out of the hospital soon after Miles and I broke up. He'd asked for me to supervise his physical rehabilitation but I got myself switched out. I'd had one conversation with him since Miles and I ended things and that was simply to tell him that it was over and he could leave me alone.

He must have thought that he'd be able to win me over or something because he'd sent me flowers and things a few times. He'd called and one time he even cornered me at the hospital to try and talk to me. I think he realized I was truly done when I wasn't even willing to argue back and forth with him. I didn't hate him; it was more of an indifference than anything. He made it clear that he was still interested in me, but I wasn't even about to entertain that.

Christian had proven to me who he was as a person. I put my foot down and let him know that while I was done with Miles, there wasn't a chance that I would ever get serious about him.

Christian hadn't believed me at first but I think he was finally starting to get the picture.

I'd been running for a few minutes as I turned down another path. The path was next to a small field filled with flowers of all different types and colors. They were absolutely beautiful. Looking at them reminded me of Miles and all the times he'd brought me flowers or little gifts.

Looking at the flowers caused my mind to travel. I was wondering where Miles was and what he'd been up to. Not hearing from him in so long had pushed him out of my mind for the most part but every now and then I'd see something that would remind me of him, and my mind would flashback to the times we'd spent together. My heart stung for a moment as I recalled him fondly. I hoped that he was alright. In my head I figured that he must have moved away. I figured it would make it easier for him to forget about me as well if he wasn't around anyone or thing that would remind him of me.

Leaving Miles hurt but I knew that ultimately it was for the best. He and I had a relationship that was built on trust, so I hoped that he trusted that my decision was only for his benefit. I didn't know what I'd do with myself if he went to jail, so I did what I had to do in order to keep him out.

About half an hour later I was stepping out of the shower and wrapping a towel around my wet body. My run had taken a lot out of me since I hadn't done it in a while but it felt good. I told myself that I needed to do more things like that—normal things that put me back on track. I'd been in a funk for a while but I was coming out of it slowly.

I wasn't scheduled to work but I was on call. I got partially dressed and headed into my living room to chill out. If my pager didn't go off within the next two hours, I was free for the rest of the day.

Well, my relaxation was pretty short lived. I got a chance to watch about half an hour of television before the pager went off and I was summoned to work. I headed in and checked in with a supervisor who informed me that Ashley hadn't come in that day so I would be dealing with her patients. I liked that the hospital trusted me enough to deal with her patients since she was a little higher up than me. However, working Ashley's patients meant that I'd be working closer with Stella. I wasn't dreading it, but we'd only really seen on another in passing. Being forced to work together meant that we would *have* to speak to one another We couldn't do our jobs otherwise.

I decided to be a professional and a grown woman about it. Stella and I had been on the outs for a while but I saw working with her as a chance for the two of us to start to build a friendship again. If it seemed like she didn't want to then I'd just keep it professional. If she was open to it, then I'd tell her that we could just take baby steps or something.

"Hello," Stella said as she came up to me. I was over at a nurses' station and had just finished speaking to one of the nurses. Stella had a slight smile on her face as she spoke.

"Hey," I said. I could tell that the two of us were feeling one another out, trying to see who would be the first one to really break the ice.

"So, you're covering for Ashley today, right?" Stella asked. I was sure that she already knew that, being that she was higher up than I was as well.

"Yeah," I answered with a nod.

"Well, this should be fun. Almost like old times," Stella added with a smirk.

"Hopefully so," I returned her smile. "Stella, since we're going to be working so closely today, I wanted to take this chance to apologize to you. I'm sorry for everything that happened before. I know that you were just trying to be my friend and I should have seen that you were just looking out for me."

I knew that the only way we'd really be able to move on would be if we got the apologies out of the way, so I just went for it. I'd had time to think and I realized that I couldn't put the blame completely on Stella. She might have gotten on my nerves with her methods, but her heart was in the right place.

Stella shook her head back at me. "No, I should be the one saying sorry. I shouldn't have put my foot in my mouth as often as I did. You're grown and at the end of the day, you know what's best for you." She took a breath and let it out in a huff. "In all honesty, I was a little jealous. You had two guys going after you and I just feel like guys don't take me serious all the time, at least not as serious as they should."

"Well, we were both wrong about some stuff.

But now that we know that, do you think we can move on?" I asked. I was smiling and got excited when she returned it.

"I would love that," she said. She walked up to me and the two of us embraced. It felt good to have my friend back again. "Go get your day started and I'll see you when we do our rounds."

"Alright, see you," I said as I broke the hug and headed off. I felt like it was a sign of possible good things to come.

## CHAPTER 20

A few days later I could say that things were really back on track, not completely, but I was starting to feel normal again. Ashley had come back to work the next day following her absence and she made a point out of thanking me for helping her out. She said that she'd heard nothing but good things about the way that I treated and cared for her patients and she was appreciative of it. I was glad for it too because it let me know that I was doing something good. After all he negativity of the last few months, I needed a change.

I was standing at the nurse's station, only

halfway paying attention to my phone as I watched one of the nurses struggle to find a patient's vein. Stella walked up to me without me noticing.

"Is she new?" she asked with a nod in the direction of the nurse.

I nodded my head. "Yeah," I said as I turned away from her to focus on Stella, "hopefully she'll get it together soon enough."

"Hopefully. It's just blood from a vein, not from a stone," she joked. I joined her in laughter. "How's your day been? Anything exciting planned for the weekend?"

Stella and I weren't back to where we were, but we'd been talking more in the last few days than we had in the last few months. We still weren't all the way back on track like we were before, but it was nice to at least not have any issues with her anymore. I liked Stella and appreciated her as a friend.

I shook my head. "No, I'm off though so I need to find something to do," I said. "Maybe I'll go out or something, I don't know. I just wanna be busy." In all honesty, I kind of hated my off days. Sitting around with my thoughts and feelings all day long wasn't working out for me. I was always trying to keep myself busy. It was the easiest way to stop myself from thinking about Miles and everything that was on my mind as far as he was concerned.

"Yeah, I don't have anything planned either," Stella said. "I was thinking of heading to my parents' house but they get on my nerves so who knows?"

"I know how that can me," I chimed in.

The elevator opposite the nurse's station dinged. The door opened and a Latino man stepped out. He was clearly a delivery person. He held a bright bouquet of flowers in his hand and was looking down at a card. He checked in with the nurse at the front of the station and handed her the flowers. She in turn got up and walked them down to us, setting them down on the counter between Stella and I and then handing me the card.

"What are these? Who would be sending me flowers?" I wondered out loud. Before I looked at the card, I studied the flowers. They were gorgeous but they weren't my favorites. Either way they were still nice. I tilted my head down some as I inhaled their intoxicating scent.

"Who are they from?" Stella pressed.

The outside of the white envelope said, "Peace Offering" and for just a few seconds, I let my mind go. My heart sped up just at the thought of the flowers being from Miles. I tore the back of the card open and turned it over to read it.

If Stella hadn't been right there, I wouldn't have said anything to her about the flowers. Still, the fact that she was hovering around meant that I couldn't ignore her. I read the letter on the card out loud.

"Let these flowers serve as a peace offering between us," I read. "Can we start fresh? I know things went south but I think we can be in a better place. Dinner tonight?" The card was signed by Christian.

Stella took the card from my hands and read through it again to herself. She smelled the flowers and then started gushing over all of it.

"Isn't this so romantic?" She beamed. "First you save his life and now he's trying to get at you again. I didn't think Christian had all this sweet stuff in him. He's something else, isn't he?"

"Yeah, he's something else alright," I said in a flat tone.

Stella might have been head over heels for Christian at the moment, but I still wasn't too sold. All too quickly my mind flashed back to everything that had happened between us. Stella might have changed her tune if she knew that Christian had been basically blackmailing Miles and I a few months ago with information that he had on us. I wasn't about to let her know any of that though.

While Stella was busy going off about Christian and his "nice" gesture, I was thinking about what to do. I was a big believer in that saying about someone showing you who they are and you believing them. Christian's true colors had been revealed and I didn't like what I saw at all. Still, now that I knew what he was capable of, I could make moves to protect myself.

"So, what are you gonna do?" Stella asked. She'd snapped me from my train of thoughts.

"About Christian?" I asked. "I was just thinking about it."

"I don't know what happened between you two, but you should at least hear him out," she suggested. "It can't hurt and even if it doesn't work out, at least you get a free outing."

I nodded my head with understanding. I

held the flowers up and looked at the card. They *were* something nice. I thought about it a little longer and then started to grin as I pulled out my phone to text Christian. I wasn't really excited about the gifts, but I put on a show for Stella's benefit.

I sent Christian a text letting him know that I would go out with him but it wasn't a date at all. He texted back saying he was glad and that I could pick the place and time. I told him that I was down to do something that same day after work. I would just go home and change my clothes before I met him. I wanted to look nice, if only to remind him of what he wouldn't be getting anymore. I could sleep with Christian from time to time, but I didn't plan on taking him seriously, not after everything that happened before.

"When are you guys going out?" Stella asked.

"I told him today," I answered. "I figure we could go out for drinks or something, nothing too much."

"That sounds like it's for the best," Stella said.

I opened my mouth to speak but at that moment, both of our pagers ended up going off. We exchanged looks with one another and then looked down at them. We were both being called to the Emergency Room, which most likely meant that something was going on that needed our attention.

Stella and I both headed downstairs. We were met by a few nurses who prepped us on the situation. We had a Level One Trauma situation coming in that would require our help. Apparently, someone had been shot a few blocks away and was losing blood rapidly. We didn't know what condition he was in, just that it was an African American male in his 20s.

Stella and I grabbed some scrubs and waited as the ambulance pulled up. The double doors that led to the E.R. burst open as the gurney carrying the person pushed through them. I couldn't see the person's face at first because I was caught off guard by the amount of blood that there was.

I moved closer to the man and was shocked that I recognized him. His name was CJ and I remembered him because he was one of Miles' security people. He'd apparently been shot 5 times and had stopped breathing.

I went into doctor mode immediately, trying my best to help him. He would need immediate surgery, so Stella made the call for someone to prep an operating room. In the meantime, him not breathing was my immediate concern. His right lung had collapsed and unless we got it inflated again, he'd most likely go brain dead from lack of oxygen. I ended up having to cut a hole in his throat and sticking a tube down it in order for him to get the air that he needed.

Hours later and CJ's situation still hadn't gotten much better. I'd managed to get him breathing again but only with the help of a machine. He'd been shot so many times that blood had been leaking from all over his body. We'd transfused him but because of the blood loss, he'd slipped into a coma. We tried to wake him but nothing worked. We kept him medicated and planned on paying close atten-tion to him. The hours after he'd come in we're touch and go, and the situation hadn't improved much from there.

It wasn't usually my job to make the calls to

a patient's family. However, I noticed after some time that no one had shown up for CJ. Whenever I noticed stuff like that I always made it my business to try and identify the next of kin. If he woke up I knew that he'd want someone to be there.

I headed to one of the computers on the floor and logged in. I searched for CJ's patient history. People probably didn't realize how far back hospital records could go. I searched for his information and saw that he'd been a patient of ours a few months back due to getting food poisoning. He'd recently changed his emergency contact to...Miles Wilson.

I stared at the name on the computer screen. Miles was the only other person listed on CJ's patient file. The number that they had for him wasn't updated but I had the right one. I couldn't believe that after so long apart, it seemed like fate would be bringing us back together.

I pushed those thoughts out of my head and remembered that I had a job to do. I didn't want to be the one to make the call. I hadn't done anything wrong by looking into CJ, as he was my patient. However, they might ask questions about why I seemed so personally involved in him and his wellbeing. Ultimately, I decided to let my supervisors know what was happening and I was going to have one of the staff nurses make the call to Miles.

I got off of the computer and headed towards the front of the large circular desk to speak to a nurse when a voice caught me off guard.

"Yo, can you tell me what room Cornell Jacobs is in?" The voice sounded frantic as it spoke.

I came around the corner to make sure that my ears weren't deceiving me. Miles was standing there at the reception desk asking for his friend. He caught me off guard because I hadn't even asked anyone to make the call yet.

"Yo," he called out as he tried to get the nurse's attention. She was on the phone with someone else and couldn't speak at the moment.

"Miles," I said in a voice loud enough for him to hear. He stopped trying to get attention and looked up at me. His eyes went blank and appeared glazed over. Our gaze went on for what seemed like forever. He finally took a few steps towards me.

"Kallie, you know anything about my friend?" he asked. The moment that had felt like slow motion seemed to speed back up. I shook my head a little bit as if I were coming out of daze.

I nodded my head. "Come on, I'll show you where he is," I said as I started to lead the way down the hall. "We did our very best for him but... he's slipped into a coma."

Miles stopped walking. He had a horrified expression on his face as he looked at me. I reached out to put my hand on his shoulder to comfort him, but I held it back. If I touched him, I might not ever want to let go.

"In all honesty, we're monitoring him very closely," I continued. "He's getting the best care that we can give him but it's up to him to fight at this point."

Miles took a deep breath and then resumed walking alongside me. "I believe you. I know you wouldn't let anything happen to a patient," Miles said.

"Here's your friend's room," I said as we

stopped at the door. "He's in a private room since so many people are in and out of there."

"Thank you," Miles said. I could tell that he wanted to say or do something more. He opened his mouth to speak and then closed it right back. He nodded at me before he headed into the room.

I stood outside of it for a little while, debating if I should go inside. I could help him feel better, I knew that much to be true. I let out a little sigh as I walked away, heading home to get ready for my outing with Christian later on that evening.

A few hours I was sitting at a table for two with Christian. I'd picked out a lounge that I'd been to a few times before. He had offered to pick me up, but I told him that I'd see myself there and back because I didn't want him to get the wrong impression about it being a date. He joked that since it wasn't a date, he wouldn't be paying. I told him that he was still on the hook for drinks because he was the one trying to apologize.

We had been there for a little over two hours and much to my surprise, I seemed to be enjoying myself. I made it clear to Christian that he was still on my shit list and he apologized over and over again. It seemed like he'd changed a little bit. He was listening to me more and wasn't acting like his usual self. I still had my guard up but I let myself enjoy his company.

"Are you having a good time?" Christian asked. He jokingly raised his hands up in surrender. "It's not a date, but I'm at least allowed to ask that, right?" He smiled at me.

Despite myself, I smiled back. "Oh hush," I joked. "Yeah, I'm having a good time."

"That's good," he replied. "Listen, I'm about to head to the bathroom. How about another round when I come back?"

I nodded my head. "Sounds good to me," I said.

Christian got up from the table and headed off towards the restroom. No sooner than I'd lost sight of him did the waiter come up to me and set a drink down on the table.

"I'm sorry, I didn't order this," I said. I grabbed the drink and tried to hand it back to him.

He kept his hand at his side and refused it, shaking his head. "There's a gentleman on the other side of the bar who said to deliver this to you. He also said I should give you this." He reached into the pocket of his apron and pulled out a small note, handing it to me.

I thanked him and quickly opened the note. I immediately recognized the scratchy handwriting.

*It was good to see you. I'm not giving up that easily.* *-Miles*

I reread the two sentences over and over again before I spotted Christian making his way back over to me. I stuffed the note into my purse before he could see it. I hadn't told Christian that I'd seen Miles earlier that day and I hadn't planned on it either. Christian and I might have been playing nice for the moment, but I wasn't about to forget that he pretty much held Miles' fate in his hands. Until it was safe, I was playing everything with him close to my chest.

"Why'd you get another drink?" Christian asked as he came back over and sat down across from me. "I thought you were waiting for me."

"You were taking too long, so I got one for myself," I teased. I sipped the drink that Miles ordered and put it back down on the table. "You should catch up."

"I'm glad to see you're loosening up," Christian said with a grin on his face. "Let me find that waiter so I can get one for myself."

An hour or so later, Christian paid the tab and we left.

***TO FIND out when Mia Black has new books available,* follow Mia Black on Instagram: @authormiablack**

ALSO BY MIA BLACK

**Loved this series? Make sure you check out more of Mia Black's series listed below:**

**Follow Mia Black on Instagram for more updates: @authormiablack**

CPSIA information can be obtained
at www.ICGtesting.com
Printed in the USA
LVHW021634120619
621003LV00013B/519